DIAMOND JOHNSON

CHAPTER ONE

Buzz! Buzz! Buzz!

That was my phone buzzing on the dresser. I wouldn't dare answer it, especially when I just got in my bed not even thirty minutes ago. I honestly felt like my phone never rang as much as it should throughout the day, but the moment I lay my head down to get some rest was when people all of a sudden wanted to engage in conversation with me.

After a few minutes of nonstop buzzing from my phone, the noise finally came to a halt. Now that I had complete silence in my room, except for the late-night Miami breeze that was coming through the open windows in my room, I took that time to close my eyes again and drift back to that place that I loved to go. That place that I would dream of going after a long day. That place was sleep.

The moment I flipped my pillow on the other side and propped it up just the way I liked it, my damn phone went to buzzing again. Sucking my teeth, I removed the eye mask that I had over my eyes, which I loved to sleep in at night, and reached over to turn on the lamp that was on the nightstand next to me. My phone was now in my hands, and I saw the name Juju, short for Juliana, flash across the screen. I released a sigh along with throwing my head back on the headrest of the bed, playing a mental battle with myself and trying to figure out if I wanted to answer the phone or not.

Juju was my fiancé, Dewayne's, cousin. I wouldn't say that I liked Juju, nor would I say that I disliked her. If anything, I just tolerated her. She had a lot of shady ways about her when it came to some of the things she would say to me, and we just didn't have that good of a connection. The shady ways would come in whenever I mentioned anything regarding Dewayne and me getting married. I could say that I wanted my wedding reception to be held at a certain hall that I knew was pretty popular in the Miami area, and she would make a comment like, "Are you sure this marriage is even going to happen?"

That was the type of statement that I was forced to put up with from her, but I just wrapped it up as her being jealous of the love that Dewayne and I shared, especially when she didn't have a man of her own. I felt like she envied the relationship that I had with her cousin. This may sound like a silly thing to say, but I also felt like at times she wished that she and Dewayne weren't blood-related just so she could test the waters and sleep with him or get some of the love and affection from him that I got. It was weird the way she loved him, but she always attributed it to her just being a very overprotective little cousin.

Juju was the only family Dewayne had that I knew of, met, or even had a relationship with, although the relationship was nowhere near strong. That was simply because when he and I met, he told me that he didn't have a relationship with the other members of his family. As he got older and started generating a lot of money from his businesses, his family began to grow jealous of him, so any relationship that he had with them was pretty much dampened.

You know those family members that you have in your life who feel that you owe them something when your hands begin to touch more money? Well, that's how he explained the members of his family to me. One would have thought that Juju would have been like that, just because of the fucked-up personality that she had, but Dewayne made it seem like Juju had never asked him for a dime in his life.

My fiancé was the very successful owner of several car rental shops throughout Miami, Miramar, and even Fort Lauderdale. It wasn't just your regular car rental shop either. They were the luxurious cars that people would dream about or dwell over in those sports magazines. I'm talking cars that would range from Rolls Royce, Lamborghini, and Ferrari, just to name a few. The minimum rate to rent a car through my fiancé's shop was $1,000. With that, you can only imagine the lifestyle that I've become accustomed to living since being with him.

Before I met Dewayne, it was just me, my oldest sister, Summer, and our mother, Sandra. We didn't have it easy growing up. In fact, I didn't get a bed of my own until I reached my early twenties, and that was after I'd saved up enough money to finally move out of Sandra's house and get an apartment of my own. You'll often hear me refer to my mother as Sandra because it was the only name that I was ever allowed to call her. It was the name that she preferred.

To this day, as a twenty-nine-year-old woman, I can't tell you what my mother did for a living when I was growing up. I could tell you the suspicions that I had of her occupation, but I was too ashamed to even let it slip from my mouth. All I knew was that when I was a little girl, and the bus would drop me off at home after school, she wouldn't be home. I usually wouldn't see her until sometime the next morning. Even when I would see her the next morning, much conversation wouldn't go on because she would be so tired from being out all night that she would be dead asleep when I got up in the mornings with Summer, who was two years older than me.

I had it hard growing up, man. My mom didn't make shit easy for us. If I wanted twenty dollars as a little girl just so I could attend a field trip with the rest of my classmates, my mom would literally make me work for it. I'm talking six years old having to wash her clothes, fold them, cook her food, clean the entire house, only to be told that she didn't have twenty dollars. At six years old, I remember like the back of my hand standing on top of a dining room chair and frying chicken over the stove for my mama.

Yes, I was only twenty-nine, but in a way, I felt double my age because I started doing things at a young age, which forced me to grow up. I knew how to separate my whites, darks, and lights in a load of laundry at six because Sandra would make me do hers. I knew how to walk to the grocery store with an EBT card in my back pocket and come back home with every single item on the list that she asked for, and I better not have come back without her lottery tickets. My mom "knew" the owner to the store, which was the only reason why my little ass was able to walk up to the counter and purchase lottery tickets.

As a kid, I was sheltered my whole life. Not because my mom was always trying to limit my exposure to the dangers of this world or keep me protected, but it was more so I could be in the house with her whenever she was home and just be her personal slave. She didn't let me do shit. There was a window back at our old house, which was right inside the kitchen. I used to sit in a wooden chair right in front of it, and for hours out of the day, I would sit with my legs pulled up to my chest and wish to be like those other kids outside playing catch, kickball, or in the summer, having on my swimsuit and playing in the water hose.

I wasn't stupid, though; I knew that my mom was only keeping me inside the house, so I wouldn't go outside and run my mouth about the ass whoppings that she would hand out to me on a regular basis. It would be damn near ninety degrees outside, and she would still send me to school in a sweater and long pants to cover up her dirty work. Regardless of how many times she would threaten me an ass whipping if I were to ever tell that she was putting her hands on me, I guess she still didn't trust that I would keep her secret safe. The only place I was allowed to ever go was to school and to the grocery store for her.

The first chance I got, which was when I turned twenty-two, I moved out. At this time, Summer was gone because she'd enlisted in the navy, so it was just Sandra and me. The physical abuse had stopped when I was probably about nineteen years old, but the verbal, the mental, and the psychological abuse remained. For months, I stacked my paycheck that I got every other week from Walmart, where I had an overnight stocking job. Eventually, I finally had enough to put down for the security deposit for a one bedroom, one bathroom apartment.

The area that I moved to was bad. For me to say that it was bad meant that it was baaddd, because I was a project baby who had lived in the hood my entire life, but this hood was much different. The gangs there pretty much ran the entire apartment complex, and shoot outs would happen in broad daylight. It took my home getting broken into while I was out working one night for me to go back to the very place that I thought I had left for good, which was Sandra's house.

Of course, I wasn't welcomed back with open arms. This time, I was forced to pay rent, and she even had me paying her car note. I had no other place to go, so I had to stay. The money I made could only afford me to live in the projects, and I was too scared to live like that on my own, so I settled for more abuse, more degradation, and simply just more of not being loved. I even settled for her taking advantage of me because when I moved back in with her, it was like she felt that I was her personal breadwinner and left all of the bills up to me.

The only thing she paid was the electric bill, which was hardly fifty dollars because Sandra wouldn't let her air run like that during the day. Half the time, the windows in the apartment stayed open, and the only TV that was in the apartment was the one she had in her room. Sandra was definitely a piece of work, but damn, she was all I had. Summer was gone, and we'd talk once a month. I had been a loner for pretty much my entire life, so I didn't have any friends. My mom was as hateful as hateful could get, but at the end of the day, she was all that I had. Sadly, I used to feel that she would be all that I would ever have.

I met Dewayne after I turned twenty-five. He came in Walmart one night. Out of all the workers that he could have asked for help finding the toiletries aisle, he asked me. I remember that night just like it was yesterday. I remember the way he looked at me as if I was the most attractive woman that he'd ever seen in his life. I didn't know if he was just acting that way because he wanted to sleep with me, because, for years, I had heard from my mom how no guy would ever be attracted to me because of the skin condition, vitiligo, that I was born with.

The condition only took up certain spots on my face,

which was right above my eyebrows, and on my ears. Further down my body was where the condition really made my self-esteem drop tremendously. It was on both of my hands, and it took up just about my entire stomach, making me look like a cow, which was the name that Sandra would call me because she knew it would hurt my feelings. It was on my thighs, legs, and even certain parts of my feet. Crazy thing is, I never minded that Sandra made me wear sweaters to school when it was scorching hot. I didn't know why she would always threaten me to not take off my sweater when that was the last thing she should have been worried about. The kids in my class would bully me or make jokes about my condition, so my sweater stayed on.

As I got older, you would have thought that I was some sort of science experiment that had gone wrong because people would point and stare, trying to figure out just what the hell was wrong with me. People were so damn misinformed when it came to my condition. I remember when I started the job interview at Walmart years ago. At the time, I was still hiding the spots on my body, so my attire for the interview had me fully clothed to the point that my condition wasn't visible. I had also applied make-up to my face, so it wasn't visible there either. The day I started the job, of course, I had to be in my uniform attire, so the spots were visible. I assumed that one of the other stock clerks had seen the spots, so they told our manager. Do you know I had to sit face to face with my manager and explain that my skin condition wasn't contagious? She feared that the other workers, herself, or even some of the customers would *catch something,* which were the words she used. For years, I felt like I was constantly explaining myself to people and letting them know that they couldn't 'catch' what I had nor was I contagious.

I didn't know if guys weren't attracted to me because of the skin condition, but Dewayne was the first guy to ever come into my life and make me feel beautiful. He was older than me, twenty-nine at the time, and it was his fascination for my 'spots' that started our relationship. He'd never seen anyone with this skin condition before, and with the way he was staring at it in amazement and telling me how beautiful it was, I finally started to accept that this was what God had given me.

Dewayne was fine! The type of fine that made me question what he saw in me. I expected him to be with someone who was drop dead gorgeous because that's what he was. Dewayne had a honey colored type of skin tone, almost to the point that his skin was golden. Perfect, short, curly hair, perfect teeth, perfect body, just perfect everything. He and I hit it off very quickly. In fact, I'm a little embarrassed to say this, but after only knowing him for a week, I lost my virginity to him in the back seat of one of his cars, which was his white Rolls Royce Wraith.

I didn't know much about men because I'd never been in a relationship with one, so I only knew about the things that I saw on TV, or that I read in books, I just assumed that after he and I had sex, he would be done with me. In fact, he did the total opposite. The next day, he had me quit my job. I moved out of Sandra's house, and she told me that I'd better not come back because she felt that I'd left her high and dry. That same year, I birthed a set of twins for him, which were now our three-year-old son and daughter, Dewayne Jr. and Storm.

A year after that, he proposed. Here we are, two years later and still engaged, but the wedding is on the way. My lifestyle had changed tremendously. I went from not having enough money, to having too much money that I didn't know what to do with myself. I no longer worked because my fiancé was the breadwinner. The only job I had was to take care of the house and the children.

In the last five years, my fiancé had introduced me to parts of the world that I could only dream about when I was younger. With his demanding career and his desire to continue expanding his empire, it caused him to be gone a lot, sometimes for weeks at a time. So, a night like tonight, with me sleeping in this big ass bed, in this big ass mansion, with my kids tucked away in their beds down the hall wasn't new to me. Many of my nights were like this. Of course, I complained, but Dewayne's answer would always be, "Would you rather me stay home with you all day and be broke?"

Sad thing is, I wouldn't mind that lifestyle. I had struggled damn near all my life, so if I had to struggle again and just get a little bit more of his time, then I wouldn't mind that at all.

"Hey," I answered, followed by a yawn because I was tired as hell.

My little three-year-olds were now going through a

phase where they didn't like going to sleep. They would fight their sleep and cry all night until they finally drifted off. Although the two of them kept me on my toes, I wouldn't have minded having more down the line, but that opportunity was stripped away from me immediately after I gave birth to the twins when Dewayne demanded that I get my tubes tied.

I remembered crying that night because I'd given birth to my twins at 11:57 P.M and telling Dewayne that I didn't want to get my tubes tied. He quickly walked over and whispered in my ear that he would walk out of that hospital room, not sign the birth certificates for our children, and would leave the three of us high and dry. So, what did I do? At the age of twenty-six, I made a permanent decision to get my tubes tied, and here I am now, not even thirty, and I would never be able to naturally have any more children.

Love made me make such a crazy decision. I loved Dewayne too much to go against his word or to put myself and our children in a position where he would leave us. That was just how Dewayne was, though. He was very controlling, but I knew he meant well. He'd never been physically abusive with me, but just like my mom, he could say some things that would really hurt. I didn't want to prove my mom right, though, which was the reason I continued to stay, although I knew that things hadn't been the same since he and I first met.

The day I left her home, she swore that he was going to start treating me like shit later on down the line, and I hate to say this, but she was right. Yes, we had our good days, and part of the reason Juju was so obsessed with having a man like mine was that Dewayne never treated me anything opposite of perfect whenever others were around to witness our love. I guess you can say we had one of those relationships where everything was good on the outside, but once you stepped foot on the inside, you would see that Dewayne and I hadn't shared the same bed in months. He hasn't touched me in months, and sadly, I hadn't seen my own fiancé in weeks!

I didn't know what changed him. Everything was damn near perfect between us during the first year that we were together. He really didn't start treating me like I was a burden until I announced that I was pregnant. Dewayne never flat out told me that he wanted me to get an abortion, but he did say little things that kind of put it in the air that abortion was the route he wanted to take. He said little things like he didn't feel that the two of us were ready to have a child together because when I got pregnant, we had only been together for three months. He even told me that it wouldn't look right for us to bring a child into this world since the two of us weren't married. He just said all the things that he felt would convince me to have an abortion, but I never made the decision to do so.

For one, it would have been selfish of me to terminate a pregnancy when I was well informed on what would happen since Dewayne and I were having sex just about every day without using any sort of protection. That is when I felt like he began to resent me. He started spending more nights away from home. Sad to say, I went through my entire pregnancy alone. I attended every single one of my prenatal appointments by myself. The birthing classes were attended by just me, and when I would go baby shopping for clothes and just anything that our babies would need, I spent that time by myself as well. Because Dewayne would give me the money to purchase the items for our twins, I guess he thought it would make up for the time that he wasn't putting in to prepare for their arrival.

So, one may want to know why the hell I would continue to stay with a man who wasn't putting in any type of effort when it came to me. The answer to that question is because this was the closest thing to love that I had ever experienced in my life. This was a perfect world for me compared to the shit that I would endure if I decided to go back home. Yes, I was ignored just about every second of the day. Yes, I was left feeling that Dewayne was cheating on me, but I could handle it, man.

Sandra had pretty much numbed me to ever feeling any type of pain in my life. Although I was engaged, and at times I felt like I was the only partner in this relationship, you better believe that I hadn't cried over this shit not once. I did enough crying when I was younger to last a lifetime, so these days, I just felt like I didn't have any more tears left to cry.

"Winterrrrr… He's gonnneee… He'sss gonneeee. My cousinnn is deaddd," Juju cried into the phone.

I rolled my eyes because Juju was so damn dramatic. The only cousin that I knew of hers was Dewayne, and I knew damn well that she wasn't calling my phone and telling me that he was dead because he was in Atlanta looking at potential properties today to open another business. I'd literally just talked to him about three hours ago because he called to check on the kids and me. Honestly, he'd just called to check on the twins. He spoke to me for literally thirty seconds, and then he had me pass the phone to the twins. Hey, he still called, right?

"Juju, what are you talking about? Who's gone?" I asked, standing up from the bed and walking into the bathroom because all of a sudden, I had a strong urge to pee.

She was taking forever to tell me who was gone; she was doing so much crying and sniffling that I'd already pissed, wiped myself, and washed my hands. The lights were on in the bathroom, shining down brightly on me so I could see myself clearly. I tried to avoid those things as much as possible. The things that I was speaking so low on were mirrors. Although I was never really best friends with a mirror because of my skin condition, I really began to become enemies with them the older I got, especially after I had the twins.

While I was pregnant, I went through a severe depression. The depression caused me to run to food, which was my comfort zone. Food was the only thing that I felt had kept me going. It was bad enough that I was already pregnant with twins, so I already knew that I would gain more weight than the average woman who was pregnant with just a single baby. In fact, I gained close to one hundred pounds when I was pregnant with the twins and was the heaviest I'd ever been in my life, which was a whopping 245 pounds.

My twins were now three years old, and I still hadn't lost all the weight that I'd gained. I went to the OBGYN a few months ago for my annual checkup, and I want to say that I was 220. My whole life, I'd always been thick, but back then, I used to like my body. I had a little waist with big thighs and legs, and my weight wouldn't go past 180. I used to have a head full of long, thick hair, but after the twins, I suffered badly from alopecia, so my hair was nowhere near as full and thick as it used to be.

In fact, just last month, I'd gone to the salon and had them cut it for me. Now, I rocked a short cut colored with honey and blonde, which had to be one of the few things about myself that I liked. My eyes were pretty too. Sandra nor Summer had these greenish, hazel colored eyes that I had, which was something that set me apart from them. If you looked really deep into my face, you could see where I had tiny freckles. Because I was walking around the house in a little cropped shirt and sweats, you could see the left-over footprints (stretch marks) that my twins had left me with. I still had the little bulge of fat on my stomach from the pregnancy, there was cellulite in my thighs, and dammit, I had to wear my good bra just about every day I went out. I breastfed my children until they were two years old, so my breast did drop a little bit in the process.

I was nowhere near perfect, and I wasn't one of those people who pretended to be. I had flaws out of this world. Sometimes, I allowed my flaws to get the best of me. They even had me believing that the physical changes that had taken place in my body were part of the reason why my fiancé now treated me as if I was the villain instead of his lover.

"Winter, Dewayne is dead. He got into a bad car accident… anddd… annddd… he's goneeee," Juju finally came back on the phone and told me.

Funny how just minutes ago, I wasn't paying her little rant any attention because I just chalked it up as her doing the most or just me simply not knowing this cousin that she spoke of. Was she talking about my Dewayne? My fiancé? The father of my children? She couldn't have been.

"Juju, what are you talking about? I just spoke to Dewayne a few hours ago, and he's in Atlanta. He literally called me as he was walking into his hotel room!" I screamed because I wanted her to know how wrong she was.

"Dewayne isn't in Atlanta, Winter. He's here! What's left of him is here," she cried.

I slouched down on the floor with the phone still glued to my ear as I took this all in. So many questions were running through my mind. How was it that there was a strong possibility that my fiancé may be dead, but the only thing I was worried about was why he would lie to me and tell me that he would be in Atlanta for the weekend? Why would he have me pack up his suitcase for the weekend with all the clothes that he would need if he were still going to be in Miami this whole time? What was the purpose of all of that? Those were the answers that I wanted.

I'd forgotten that Juju and I were even on the phone

because she was left with her thoughts, and I was left with mine.

"Look, Winter, I only called you so that you could be aware of what was going on. You cannot come down here. It wouldn't be a good look, and—"

"What the fuck are you talking about, Juju? What do you mean it wouldn't be a good look? This is my fiancé that we are talking about. I've spent the last four years with this man, and we share two children. Fuck whatever look you're talking about. If Dewayne is gone like you say he is, then I'm more qualified than you or anyone else to be wherever he is right now. Now, where the hell is he?" I barked into the phone.

This loud, obnoxious person that I was right now was completely out of my element. I was the quiet type; sometimes I was so damn quiet that you would forget that I was even in the room. Not much would make me get out of character because I was usually the type to brush things off, even if it killed me to do so. At this point, I was no longer sitting down on the cold, tile floor. I'd stood up and was pacing the massive master bathroom while waiting for answers from Juju.

"We're at Memorial Regional. Winter, I just want you to know that I'm sorry. It just was never my place to tell you," she said, and I ended the phone call because I didn't need anything else from her.

I kept the sweats that I was wearing on and just went inside the walk-in closet and grabbed the first sweater that I could find along with some running shoes. I removed the

Louis Vuitton headscarf from around my head and combed through my short cut then I grabbed my purse. Next, I went down the hall to the kid's bedroom. I moved like a thief in the night as I grabbed them both up from their twin-sized beds and slipped their sweaters on along with their sneakers. Then, like the supermom that I knew I was, I carried both of them out of the room on either shoulder and made my way down the stairs with them.

I used the door downstairs, which would lead me to the garage, and I went in the direction of my Mercedes Benz GlC300. I had to put my son down in order for me to put Storm in her car seat. Once she was in, then I was able to put DJ in his.

One would think that I would be a total wreck right now and could hardly function, but I was keeping it together. A big part of me was still lingering on the missing answer as to why my fiancé was really in Miami this whole time when he left yesterday, telling me that he would be in Atlanta for the next few days.

CHAPTER TWO

AT THE HOSPITAL

It was the middle of the night, going on 3:00 A.M. for that matter, so there were plenty of parking spots available. I quickly pulled my car into the available spot that was the closest to the emergency door and cut the car off. Grabbing my purse, I looked in the rearview mirror, only to see that DJ was wide awake while his sister was sleeping hard.

My twins looked identical. Although they were different genders, I swear if my eyes weren't working as efficiently as they should be, I'd get them mixed up. They both had long, thick hair, making them look like miniature versions of myself and just the newer version of how I looked when I was younger. Because DJ's hair was so long and thick and I kept it in braids, or on days when his hair wasn't done, I'd put it in a ponytail, he would often get mistaken for a little girl. My kids were every spitting image of me and had just gained little things from their father like their light brown eye color and his caramel colored skin.

"Where we at, Mommy?" DJ asked me now that I had the back door open and was unbuckling his car seat.

"It's where are we," I corrected him. My kids were only three, but I was nipping little bad habits now in the bud like improper grammar, so when they were older, those little habits wouldn't become big habits. "We're at the hospital. We're getting ready to see what's going on with Daddy. Stay right here while I get your sister, okay?" I asked, and he nodded his little head up and down as he rubbed his sleepy eyes.

He stayed right beside me like I asked while I turned my back for a second to get Storm out of her car seat. Dewayne hadn't done a damn thing physically to help me in my pregnancy, but the day I had the twins, he was the one who had come up with the name Storm. I had Serenity in mind, but, for whatever reason, I liked Storm. Of course, I questioned him on the significance of naming her Storm, and he simply told me that it was different, and he felt like it was fitting and beautiful. It wasn't until my daughter turned two that I actually began to break down the meaning of her name. I mean, we all knew what a storm was, but did we *really* know what it meant? They say a storm is a tumultuous reaction or in some cases can even be an uproar. Was an uproar on its way? What about a controversy? I often found myself questioning that over the years, but like I did everything else, I convinced myself that I was probably putting too much thought into it.

I finally had Storm out of the car, and I carried her in my arms while she lay her head on my shoulder. I used my free hand to hold onto DJ's hand. We walked with purpose into the hospital, and it didn't take but a few seconds for me to speak with the receptionist up front and tell her who I was there to see then have my photo taken for the visitor's badge.

"What's wrong with Daddy, Mommy?" my son finally asked me once the doors to the elevators had closed, and it was just the three of us on it.

I looked down at him as he looked back at me with those big, brown eyes and pulled him close. He rested his little head on my thigh.

"We're about to find out right now," was all I had for him.

The doors to the elevators finally opened, and we stepped off. As soon as we hit the corner, I saw a family room. I was going to keep walking, but I saw a face that was all too familiar, so I stopped in my tracks. It had to have been over twenty people in that family room, and out of the twenty, I only knew one. I stood by the door, pulling my son closer to me and placing the other free hand on the back of my daughter's head. I was confused.

What put me in the state of confusion was the look of shock that was on Juju's face. As if she didn't think that I was going to come down there for real. Her eyes were bloodshot red, more than likely from all the crying that she'd done, but never mind that, who were all of these people? Why did I just look at two grown men in this room who resembled my fiancé to the core? Why was there a woman in the room who was crying the way that I should have been crying? She was holding a little baby in her arms who didn't even look to be two weeks old yet. The woman who was crying and holding onto the baby was breathtakingly beautiful. She reminded me of Jennifer Lopez in her younger days. Three children sat next to her, who were very well behaved, and just like my son, they all looked sleepy as hell.

"Juju, what's going on?" I asked.

When I did, every head in the room turned to me and looked down at my children. I felt like an outcast; my children and me. I didn't know what was going on, but something told me that Juju knew these people. These weren't just people in there waiting to visit their loved ones while Juju was from a different family and waiting to view her loved one. They all had to have been connected. Something told me that they were all there to see the same person. So, again, who the hell were these people?

"Let me speak to you outside, ma'am," Juju said. She walked over and tried to grab my arm, but I shoved her off me.

For one, she was grabbing me by my arm as if she was

trying to hide me from something. And why the hell was she calling me ma'am when she knew my damn name? I always thought that Juju was a little off, maybe even a little slow. But, damn, she just called me by my name not even an hour ago, so why was I ma'am all of a sudden?

"Juliana, who is this? Why would you think it's okay to bring your little friend and her kids here for family business? For goodness sake, my fuckin' husband has just died in a damn car accident! What the hell is wrong with you, Juliana?" the Jennifer Lopez lookalike spat as she stood up from her chair with the baby in her arms.

Her body put mine to shame. Here she was with a newborn, and she looked as if she could have her own fitness DVD, even with her postpartum body. It was going on three years for me, and I still had my baby fat from the twins. It was what she said, though, that had me breathing a sigh of relief. Leave it to Juliana to have me walking into a room with another family while they were going through something like this. My crazy ass thought that these were Dewayne's family members for a second. I even convinced myself that these two fine ass men looked like him.

This woman was screaming about the death of her husband, which didn't have anything to do with me, especially when I had a man of my own. Kind of ironic, though, that her husband and my fiancé might have both died on the same night in a car accident.

"Juju, I'll leave. Which room is Dewayne in? I wish you would have stopped me when I walked in and told me that I was in the wrong room. Where is he?" I asked.

She played with her fingers while looking down at the pink and white Converse sneakers that were on her feet. I saw a tear fall from her eyes, and it hit the floor. Again, all eyes were on me in the room. Juju was acting weird as hell for some reason. You would have thought that her ass had gone deaf by the way that she was ignoring all my questions.

"Why are you inquiring about my husband? Who the hell are you?" the woman asked me.

I was confused. I mean, high school calculus confused.

"Maybe we're talking about the wrong guy. I'm here to see what's going on with my fiancé, Dewayne Washington. Tell her, Juju," I said to Juju, and she didn't say anything.

Her head was still down, and she was all of a sudden acting as if her mouth didn't work when any other time, we couldn't get her to shut up.

"I don't know what trap house, dumpster, or whatever the hell it is that you just popped out from, but if I were you, I would get the fuck out of here. My husband doesn't have a fuckin' fiancée! He has a fuckin' wife that's standing right here and four beautiful children. One of which I just gave birth to six days ago! I don't know what type of mental health issues you have, but sweetheart, look at you and then look at me! My husband would never! You better leave before I hurt your feelings," she said.

I could tell that my son was scared because he had his little arm wrapped around my thigh, and he was holding onto me for dear life, but I wouldn't dare leave because I wanted answers. I wanted answers right fuckin' now!

"Juju, you need to speak the fuck up now and say something because at this point, my word is all I have, and that doesn't seem to be enough. Tell her how I've been in Dewayne's life for the past four years! Tell her that these are his kids! You were there when I gave birth to our twins. You've been there since the beginning!" I said to Juju, screaming for her to have my back in this.

"Listen, I don't know who you are or how the hell you know me, but you need to leave. This is family business. Dewayne is my cousin, and this is Camila, who is the only woman in Dewayne's life. The only woman who has ever been in his life. You need to get the hell out" Juju said.

I couldn't believe this shit. I looked at Juju with shocked eyes. She was really standing here pretending to not know who the hell I was. I had known this dumb ass girl for almost five years. Granted, she and I had never been the best of friends, and I always felt like we just tolerated each other out of respect for Dewayne, but damn, never in a million years would I have thought that she would throw me under the bus like this.

I was standing there with wild eyes that were basically screaming for Juju to admit that she was just playing around and that she really knew who I was, but she quickly turned her head from me to avoid eye contact, and all I could do was shake my head. This bitch was fuckin' pathetic. Since she wouldn't have my back, I knew then that it was time for me to resort to plan B. I reached into my back pocket and pulled out my phone. I quickly went to my photos because I'd be damned if I stood here in front of all of these people and looked crazy. I had all types of proof in my phone that I knew Dewayne, and I wasn't some psycho who was out of touch with reality.

154 photos. I had an iPhone 8 plus with over 2,000 pictures in my phone since I had the 254 GB, but suddenly, all of my photos of my children were gone. I literally stood there with my phone in my hand, trying to find something, but every single picture that was in my phone of Dewayne, myself, and our children were gone. I couldn't find anything. I tried to go to the settings so I could use the iCloud as back up, but it was all of a sudden telling me that my passwords were wrong. I smiled when I realized that I had pictures in my email. I quickly exited the settings app and tried to log into my yahoo email, but I got the same thing, which was it notifying me that my password was wrong. How the hell didn't I notice that my wallpaper on my phone had been changed?

Just a few days ago, my wallpaper was a picture of the twins that I'd taken of them a while back while they were sleeping. Now, all of a sudden, my wallpaper was of some damn palm trees. What the fuck was going on? Why didn't I have proof of anything?

"Look, I don't know what's going on with my phone, but all of my pictures with Dewayne and our kids have been suddenly deleted. I have pictures at home that I can get you proof of. I have no reason to lie. You and I may not look the same, but you have to believe me when I say that Dewayne and I have been in each other's lives for the past four years. Just like you didn't know about me, I didn't know a damn thing about you. Dewayne never, I mean never, mentioned anything about you. His birthday is on February 25th. His favorite food is spaghetti. He's allergic to peanuts, cranberry, and the only milk that he can drink is soy milk because anything else will make him break out in hives.

"His favorite team is the Lakers. His shoe size is ten and a half, but depending on the brand, sometimes he can be an eleven. He writes with his left hand. Ask me whatever the hell you want to know about that man, and I will tell you. What am I going to gain from this, huh? You really think that I would come all the way down here and embarrass myself like this in front of my kids? In front of my kids, really?" I screamed at 'the wife,' and my voice even cracked a little bit because I was so pissed off.

She handed her child to an older looking woman and then walked over to me. Again, her eyes were bloodshot red, and I could see just how physically tired she was just by looking her in the eyes. I swallowed the lump that was beginning to form in my throat because I didn't have the slightest clue what she was getting ready to say.

The other people in the room were staring as if they were front and center at a Madea play.

"Let's say that you are right. Just for one fuckin' second, I'm going to entertain everything you just said to me, although I know that it's bullshit. We're talking about a man who gets up every morning to take three of our children to school before he heads into work. We're talking about a man who I sleep with five days out of the week because business forces him to travel a lot, but even that small gap of him traveling doesn't add up to him having an entire fuckin' fiancée on the side with two damn kids who look nothing like my damn husband!

"How dare you bring your ass in here and do this shit in front of my family? In front of my fuckin' kids. How dare you! My kids think the world of their father, and I will not allow you to say anything else about him that will tarnish his name or his character. Look around you, sweetie. Everyone in here is Dewayne's family. These are his brothers, behind me are his parents, his aunts and uncles are in here, his little cousins, his kids, yet all of them are looking at you the same way that I'm looking at you! How can you even believe in that crazy ass head of yours that you are his fiancé when you never even met his family? Out of respect for your kids, I think you should leave," she spat, but I wouldn't give up. I just couldn't.

"Is there a problem in here? We're getting complaints that there is a lot of commotion in this room. I'm going to ask that you all keep it down, or else you'll be forced to leave," a security guard came into the room and said.

I looked at him briefly and then turned my eyes on the culprit in front of me, looking at me with hate in her eyes, which I was sure matched the look that I was giving back to her ass. She could stand there and be as mad as she wanted to be, but her hurt couldn't even begin to compare to what the hell I was feeling right now. She was standing in a room filled with people who more than likely were going to give her all the support, comfort, and love that she needed, while the only people I had to comfort me was going to be my kids. My kids who were with me right now witnessing this whole damn thing unfold.

"I was under the impression that he didn't have a relationship with you all! That's what was told to me!" I screamed, sounding like a crazy person.

Now that everything was coming out of my mouth, I was beginning to look and sound like the fool that Dewayne had made me be for years.

"Ma'am, let's go! I just asked that you all keep it down, and you did the complete opposite of that. Let's go." The security guard came over and grabbed my arm.

I all of a sudden grew the strength of a giant because I pushed his ass off me.

"Don't touch me! Don't you dare fuckin' touch me!" I screamed, trying to back away from him, all the while grabbing my son and pulling him closer to me.

Both of my kids were hysterically crying, and I was sure it had a lot to do with seeing me out of character. I had never in my life acted like this, but I couldn't even begin to explain how hurt I was. I couldn't even explain the way my heart was stinging at the moment.

"Get your ass out of here. We just lost a loved one, and we shouldn't have to deal with this madness," one of the family members screamed.

I was screaming at just about everyone in the room, letting them know just how they had to believe me and how everything that I said was true. Before I knew it, I was thrown to the ground with the security damn near on top of me, putting all of his weight on me and trying to get me to calm down.

"Mommmmyyy... Mommyyyy... stoppp... stoppp!" both of my kids cried and screamed at the top of their lungs.

Seeing them cry and have to witness this shit was the only thing that got me to calm down. Another security guard came into the room, and it took the two of them to escort my children and me out of the room. I was so fuckin' disappointed in Juju because she had so many chances to step in, but she never did.

During the ride down on the elevator with the security, they looked at me with nothing but sympathy in their eyes, and I hated that because I couldn't stand for someone to have pity on me. I could have easily been arrested tonight, but something told me that they didn't go to those extreme measures because they genuinely just felt bad for me. The whole ride down, my throat was burning something serious because I was struggling to keep myself from crying. I wouldn't dare break down in front of these complete strangers.

"You don't have to walk with me outside. I'm fine," I said the second the elevator doors opened.

I didn't even look at them to see their reaction because I had already seen enough. I'd already made a big enough fool of myself tonight, so I didn't need to have them stick around anymore and witness me in such a vulnerable and embarrassing state. I grabbed both of my kids' hands, and I speed walked with them to the car. They were still a total wreck, but I was somehow able to tune them out.

Once I had the two of them buckled in their car seats, I went ahead and got in my seat, making sure to lock the doors. As soon as it was just us, in the comfort of our own vehicle, my fist banged repeatedly on the steering wheel.

"How could you do this to meeeee? How could you do this to our kidsssss? Whyyyy? I didn't do anything to you! A wife? Four kids? One of which you just had a week ago. Why meeee, God? Why meeee?" I cried, bringing my head down on the steering wheel and crying my eyes out.

I heard movement in the backseat, and that's when I noticed that both of my children had made their way out of their car seats and climbed up front with me. DJ got in the passenger seat while Storm climbed over and got in my lap. Seriously, no words were spoken between the three of us. None. It was like God himself had whispered to my children and told them that the only thing I needed right now was some love, and that's what they gave me.

My daughter's arm was wrapped around me, and DJ's arm was on my back as he moved his hand around in a circular motion. Funny how I was the mother, the one who was supposed to have the superwoman cape and always be strong for my children, but I was at my lowest right now. My babies, who were too damn young to even know what was going on had to be my strength. It was always me who made sure that I was their strength whenever they were crying or fussy, and now look at how the roles have changed.

My cries were the only sound in the car. I looked at my daughter, and it hit me why my fiancé had named her

Storm. The uproar had for damn sure happened tonight, and who would have known that this man was trying to warn me three years ago that a Storm was coming our way? I was just so naïve that I looked at the name in its uniqueness and not it's definition.

CHAPTER THREE

"Yooo, get up! You gotta get up out of here, shorty," was the first thing that came out of my mouth this morning when I woke up and saw that I still had little mama in the bed with me from last night.

This shit was so unlike me. I never did shit like this because once the semen ejaculated from my dick, I was kicking these bitches out the door. It wasn't on no rude shit either because I was very upfront when it came to women. If all I wanted from you was to get my dick sucked, then I made it known. If all I wanted from you was some pussy, I made that known too. I never gave these women a reason to catch feelings or to tell me that I led them on because everything was always laid out on the table before they could even drop their panties for me.

Shorty was all tangled up in the sheets and snoring like a grown ass man getting some good sleep in when I started shaking her and telling her to get her ass up. I was calling her shorty and lil mama because, for the life of me, I just couldn't remember her name. I wanted to say she said Veronica or some shit. Nah, I think she said April. I wasn't sure. All I knew was she had some fire head with some mediocre pussy. It wasn't worth the nut.

I fell asleep with this broad, and she could have set my ass up, had some niggas run up in the spot and rob me, all because I got caught slipping and let her ass spend the night. If I was going to die over some pussy, at least the pussy should have me going to sleep sucking on my thumb like a damn baby or some shit. Then again, who am I kidding? Nobody was about to rob me. Shorty didn't even have her phone on her.

All electronics were confiscated at the door because I couldn't trust these bitches. I had witnessed too many niggas from around the way get caught slipping from bringing a bad bitch home with them. Next thing they know, some niggas with masks run up on him while he got his dick all out, demanding that he cough up the money. I wasn't going out like that, so every time a bitch came over, I locked her shit up until it was time for her to leave the premises.

The spot we were at right now was called the nut house. I called it that for one reason, and one reason only; I caught my nut there, and then I was back on my way home to my castle. I could count on one hand the number of people who knew the location of that castle because it was where I lay my head at night.

The old heads from the hood had taught me years ago to never let an outsider know where you lay your head, and to always have four eyes on you; two in the front and two in the back. Also, if you didn't want no bitch calling you up and talking about she's pregnant, then you better wrap that dick up twice because no pussy in this world was tight enough or wet enough to have me wanting to become a baby daddy to a bitch that I barely even knew.

Those were just a few of the things that I learned in the hood as a child. I won't tell everything because we'll be here all day, and some of the tips and shit that I have is shit that you can't get for free. You'd have to pay me for some of this inside scoop.

"Why you so heartless, Boss? Like, damn, can I at least wash my ass first and brush my teeth before you go kicking me out? Damn!" she fussed as she sat up in the bed.

She pulled the covers from over her body, and there she sat, butt ass naked with probably the prettiest set of titties that I had ever seen in my damn life. Shorty was fine, man. She had bright red hair that I knew was all hers because last night when I was digging in her shit from the back, I had my hands all in her hair and pulling at it. A track never slipped, so I knew it was hers. She had a cute little Coca-Cola shaped frame, some pretty teeth with a small gap on the top row, and a skin tone that was so bright that she almost looked white.

I met her last night when I was at the bar after having a long ass work day. She walked right up to me and didn't have a problem letting me know that she knew who I was and that she wanted to fuck me to see if my dick was as good as the other bitches said was. If shorty didn't have any respect for her damn self, why should I take it easy on her the next morning? Fuck was I supposed to do? Wake her up with breakfast in bed? I didn't even keep water in this bitch, that's how you know that I came there to strictly fuck. She made it clear to me last night that all she wanted was some dick, so why all of a sudden did her values change?

"I'm not heartless, ma. Just straight to the point. I would have been heartless if I nutted last night and kicked you out. My heart ain't that cold, sweetheart. I let you stay all the way until 6:00 A.M, plus I didn't take the condom off last night and bust on your face like I initially wanted to. I got some heart in me. Get up, though. I got shit to take care of," I let her know as I stood up from the bed.

My dick went to swinging, almost feeling like a third leg. Just like I knew they would, her eyes left my face and fell on my dick. My Versace robe that was laid out at the foot of the bed, I grabbed it and wrapped it around my body.

"You do know that it's okay to catch feelings for me, Boss? Why are you so against love?" she asked, all of a sudden sounding like a therapist and not the same woman who had my dick so far in her throat last night that I thought she was trying to take it home with her and save some for later.

I thought about her question for a few seconds. It wasn't that I was against love or no shit like that because I had been in love before. Deeply in love before with my ex-fiancé, Amari. We had ourselves a ghetto, hood type of love. I had known her since I was nine years old and didn't know shit about love, but I knew at nine that I loved the fuck out of her. That girl was my everything, man. Beautiful, classy, funny, smart as hell, just everything that a guy would look for in a girl.

From the time we were nine until we were like sixteen, I guess you can say that it was puppy love. That's what the people from around the hood would call it since we were so young, and they felt like we didn't know shit about love. Little did they know, Mari and I had been fuckin' on each other since we were twelve, but we let them think that the shit was innocent.

When we were younger, she lived three houses down from me so we would see each other just about every day. I loved Amari because she loved a nigga when I didn't have shit. Fuck, I hated to sound like every other nigga in Miami growing up, but I had it bad, especially in my childhood. Yeah, I had both parents in the house, but that didn't mean shit because my ole boy used to beat the fuck out of my ole girl for breakfast, lunch, dinner, snack, late night snack, and midnight snack. It kills me when I hear niggas say that they wish they had their old boy in the house with them when they were growing up because it depends on what type of daddy they were looking for.

I had the type of daddy who was there for every event that I attended, cooked food for us at least two times a week, yet the nigga still wasn't shit. He was controlling like a motha fucka. I literally used to sit there as a little boy and listen to this man tell my mama how she should wear her hair to work, what shoes she should wear, and just controlling shit like that.

I was a rebellious lil nigga, so I stayed getting my ass beat. I could breathe too loud, and I had to come up out of my clothes, turn around, and put my hands on the wall while I stood there and got the shit beat out of me like I was a damn slave. I had an older sister whose name was Ocean, and a little sister, whose name was Queen. At the time, it was myself, Ocean, and my ole girl who used to get the shit beat out of us all the time by my ole boy. Out of all of us, my ole girl and I were neck and neck with who would get it the worst.

To this day, I believed that the only reason Queen didn't used to get beat the way that we did growing up was that she was still a baby. Had my ole girl stayed a little longer and allowed Queen to grow older in my house, there is no doubt in my mind that she would have had a story to tell this day about how our ole boy was physically abusive to her as well. In all honesty, Queen not having to endure the physical pain that we did or even be old enough to remember it was one of the reasons why her ass was so spoiled.

I'm not complaining about it because, at the end of the day, that was my little sister, and I wouldn't have even wanted her to go through some shit like that. Hell, I didn't want my ole girl or Ocean to have to go through it either, but I was still a kid at the time, so there really wasn't much that I could do in the first place.

One would think that with the way my ole boy was beating our ass, my ole girl would have left, but she didn't. She didn't have to explain to me why she stayed. The physical abuse really didn't start until my mom lost her job. For fifteen years, my ole girl worked as a housekeeper at a motel. The motel had gone out of business, so it forced all of the workers to be without a job.

It's like my ole boy started resenting my ole girl when she lost her job, which is why he did some of the hateful shit that he would do to her over the years. Once she was let go, we pretty much had to fully rely on my ole boy's income from doing car maintenance. He brought his ass home every day looking around to find one thing out of order. Once he found it, everybody got beat.

I know my ole girl stayed because she was thinking logically. She knew that she couldn't just pack up in the middle of the night with three kids and take us somewhere when she didn't have any money. My ole girl got pregnant her senior year in high school with Ocean, so when she took a break from school, it ended up being a permanent break, and she never went back. Without a high school diploma, she couldn't find no fuckin' job that would allow her to take care of three kids on her own, so she stayed. The only reason she was able to get that job at the motel was that she knew one of the workers there, and they looked out.

When I was fifteen years old, Ocean was eighteen. She brought her ass home one night, and the dummy didn't even try to hide the big ass hickey that was on her neck. My ole boy flipped out, and right in the middle of our living room, he slammed my big sister down on her head and beat her ass like she was a nigga, even breaking her arm in the process.

I was only fifteen, still a little nigga at the time, but had the heart of a giant, so I jumped in and fucked him up as best as I could. I fucked around and got my jaw broken that night. It took my ole girl having two kids to suffer from a broken arm and one with a broken jaw for her to leave that crazy nigga alone. Well, she didn't have much of a choice because the neighbors heard the noise, and before we knew it, police were at the door, and my ole boy was arrested.

We didn't even stick around for the nigga to get out because as soon as he was hauled off to jail, my ole girl took his car, and we left. That night, we ended up going to the hospital, and when we left, my mom checked the four of us into a homeless shelter. We had to have stayed there for a few months. During our time there, my ole girl had found a housekeeping job at another hotel, and at the same time, she was going to school for her GED.

Me, I picked up a hustle of my own. I was so fuckin' tired of struggling. Fifteen years old with an appetite out of this world, so I wanted to fuckin' eat! So, I let the white boys from my school talk me into credit card fraud. The shit was dangerous as hell, but I felt like I needed to step up and be the man in the family since my bitch ass daddy couldn't be it! I had sisters that I needed to provide for and a mother who needed help.

It was just supposed to be a one-time thing because I found out that with one card alone, I could make at least 10,000 dollars. I felt like that was all I would need, but that shit became addictive. My first run with it, I actually made fifteen thousand dollars. It was actually more than that, but Luis, who was my friend at the time, his big brother was the one coaching us to do it and stuff. So, he had to get his half of everything we made. Mannn, you'd be surprised at how easily we could get a person's credit card information.

Luis was a professional scammer, so all we really needed was a major credit card. Luis would send me and his little brother, Mathew, on little runs throughout the day for us to get people's credit card information. The biggest trick of them all was standing behind someone in the grocery line while they had their card in their hands waiting to swipe it. I could remember the sixteen-digit numbers on the card plus the expiration date along with the three numbers on the back so I would take the info back to Luis, and just that fast, I was making money.

Another thing we did was ear hustle. I was still living in the projects where the walls were very thin, so if a motha fucka from next door sneezed, I could yell back and tell them bless you. I used to ear hustle on my neighbors, and if they would order food or something, from the wall, I'd just mentally store the credit card number in my head. Again, I would give the numbers back to Louis.

After the first run that I made, I brought all the money back that Louis had given me to my ole girl, and she beat the black off my ass. I swear she beat me worse than the way my ole boy used to because she thought that I'd robbed a bank. When I told her how I actually got the money, she beat me some more, because to her, I was still stealing from people. I was still fifteen and had to live in her house and under her rules, but her telling me that I better stop what I was doing was just something that I couldn't obey.

I now knew what it felt like to make thousands in under one hour, so there was no way I could stop, especially when she was still struggling. My mom had given me the nickname Boss since I was a baby. She said that I was a bossy baby who liked to have things my way or the highway. That mentality had remained as I grew up, which was why I didn't know why she was acting so shocked that I was taking matters into my own hands, especially since I knew that we were still struggling.

I remember her looking me in my eyes and telling me that if I were to ever get caught and they took me to jail for it, she wouldn't even come down to visit me. My ole girl told me that she wouldn't even pick up the damn phone if I tried to call her. I believed her too, but I still took that risk.

What set me apart from Mathew and Luis was that I moved in silence with my money. Every dime I made went into the mattress of my bed. I was giving my ole girl money, which would just come back to me because, in her words, she didn't want any of my dirty money.

I was an older nigga now, graduated from high school, and I was still living dangerously, but one would never know because I still was moving like I was broke. I still wore dirty shoes, rocked the same outfits each week, and still slept in the same bed as my ole girl. Around this time, my ole girl had received her GED, yet she was still doing housekeeping at the hotel.

On her 41st birthday, I gave her the surprise of a lifetime, and even she couldn't turn down the gift that I was able to give her with dirty money. For years, my ole girl had been talking about opening a homeless shelter for women, but she didn't think she would be able to do it because she didn't think that she would be able to come up with the money.

In addition to the money that I'd given her for her birthday so that she could purchase the property, I told her that I would walk away from what I was doing. Not because I felt like I had enough money because there was never too much money to have, but because reality hit me, and I knew that I wanted to be around to for my family. If I were to get busted for credit card fraud, my black ass was going down.

At the time, I wasn't just the runner anymore. I was actually alongside Luis in his basement with about ten laptops surrounding us as we did what we were doing to get the money. Mann, the shit that we had on those laptops could get us buried under the jail.

I was still in a relationship with Amari at the time, and

we had a two-bedroom apartment together. She was attending college locally and seeing her get up to go to college had motivated me to go because I wasn't a dumb nigga. I knew what I wanted to do once I got my degree, and I knew what I wanted to buy too.

It took me eight years to receive my master's degree, and once I received it, I knew that I was going to be a problem for these niggas. Not only did I have the street smarts, but I had the book smarts to add on. That dirty money that I used to stash under the mattress came in handy for me. I met with a realtor the day after I graduated college and gave him a duffle bag filled with cash to purchase the run down, low income apartment homes in one of the grimiest parts of Miami. The complex had been closed down about two years ago but was now for sale.

Once it was purchased, I had all fifty apartments remodeled, which took about a year. When they were done, people were damn near pulling all-nighters outside the building, trying to be the first to move in. I was the owner of this apartment complex for a year when I started thinking about expanding. In another two years, I had brand new, luxury townhomes built right in the heart of Miami, which housed hundreds of tenants. Low income, poverty-stricken tenants.

It meant a lot to me to give back to the hood because, as a little nigga, I was constantly waiting for that one person to give back to us. They weren't calling me Boss for no reason. I was filthy rich, making my money the legal way now, and I never wanted to have to experience what it felt like to be broke again. Ever!

I was thirty-two years old now, wealthy, with plenty of businesses to my name. I had my ole girl and my two sisters, but deep down inside, I hadn't been the same in five years. I know ya'll probably wondering why I brought up Amari for that quick second and stopped talking about her. Truth is, Amari will forever be a sensitive subject for me.

I was at the peak of my career, having just purchased another property where I was having new condos built out on Miami Beach when I received the phone call from the hospital. I'd literally just put the fuckin' ink on the paper to sign my name on the dotted line and was getting ready to go home to my eight-month pregnant fiancée and share the good news when this shit happened. I got a phone call from the hospital telling me to come down because it was an emergency. I got to the hospital, only to find out that a single bullet hole to the head had killed my fiancée, and multiple shots to the stomach had killed my seed.

Five years later, and no one still knew who the fuck had killed my girl and my child. Emotionally, hell even psychologically, do you know what that type of shit can do to a human being? Right before the incident happened, I had literally just gotten off the phone with Amari. I told her that I had a surprise for her when I got home, and in the blink of an eye, I'd lost her. I'd lost my daughter. A daughter that I couldn't wait to meet. A daughter whose Disney Princess themed room was already decorated for her and just waiting for her to grace this world with her presence.

Yeah, during my younger years, I was living foul and taking from others, but did a nigga like me deserve to have my fiancée and my baby killed in broad daylight like that? I was trying to right my wrongs these days by giving back to the community, paying my tithes in church, and feeding the homeless, but I felt like none of that shit would ever be enough to make me invisible to bad shit happening in my life.

So, back to the question that I was just asked a few minutes ago. It wasn't that I didn't believe in love, but I just knew better. I put myself out there one time and look what happened. I was still suffering behind that shit, so I'll never allow another woman to get that close to my heart only to be taken away from me. From that point on, it was just strictly sex with these bitches.

"Look, a nigga didn't wake up this morning to play Dr. Phil nor Iyanla fix my life. All of these questions are going to have you standing at the bus stop and catching the bus home instead of me be a gentleman and ordering you an Uber that can take you wherever you want to go. It's your pick, sweetheart. Which one you going to choose?" I asked now that my robe was on and I had tied the knot in the front because shorty was looking at my dick like it belonged to her.

Not one time did I tell her last night that this was her dick. I could tell that I pissed her off because she snatched her clothes up that were laying on the floor next to the foot of the bed and hauled ass out of the room and down the hall to the guest bathroom. Now that she was out of the room, I walked into the bathroom that was in my bedroom. First thing I did was look at myself in the mirror. Not on no conceited shit or anything like that; if anything, just admiring the growth, man.

Years ago, when I was a little nigga, I went through that phase of thinking it was cool shit to be rocking pull out golds in my mouth. I had them on both the top and the bottom. Growing up, I had long hair, so the majority of the time, my hair was in braids that I would get done once a month, sagging pants, and all of that other ghetto bullshit. Look at me now. I took that bullshit out of my mouth and flashed the sparkly white, straight teeth that God Himself had blessed me with.

As I smiled at my reflection, I saw those deep ass dimples that I had in my cheeks, which always made the bitches go crazy. I had a dark brown skin complexion. Myself, my sisters, and my mom had the same dark brown complexion that looked good on us. I didn't have many tattoos aside from the word *Boss* that was tatted on my fist in bold font, and I had a big shoulder piece that started on my chest and took up the majority of my shoulder. It was a tribal piece that I thought was dope as fuck and had taken me three sessions to finish because of all the detail involved.

I was a solid nigga, weighing 230 pounds of pure muscle, and I stood about 6'5", so you could only imagine the many ways that I could use my strength to knock a nigga out. My ole girl liked to joke from time to time and call me a hood Ghost from the popular show *Power* because I was just as wealthy as him, and I was always in a suit, due to business. I really didn't like to compare myself to any man, but Ghost was aight. I felt like he was lame as fuck, though, for cheating on his beautiful, black wife to go and be with Angela, though.

You can call me a hoe right now only because I wasn't in a relationship, but once I was fully devoted to someone, I swear I only had eyes for them. If Amari were here right now, she would be able to vouch for that.

"Here. Go ahead and put the address in to where you need to be," I said when I walked back into the bedroom.

She was fully dressed and just sitting at the foot of the bed. I'd already showered and everything, so now I was in my boxers, my wife beater, and holding a burgundy three pieced suit in my hands. Shorty took the phone from me, keyed in whatever address she needed to on Uber, and after a few more minutes, she handed me back the phone. I saw that her Uber was only ten minutes away, and I smiled because that left just six hundred seconds with her ass in my sight. Because I wanted to be clear that I didn't want any talking between the two of us, I turned on my Bluetooth speakers and let some old school Dr. Dre play.

When she realized that she wasn't getting any attention from me, she finally stood up from the bed, grabbed her purse, and walked out of the room. Over the loud music, I heard the front door slam, and that's when I walked over to the window, and I saw that she was getting into the Uber. Little bitch didn't even say thank you!

In another twenty minutes, I walked out the front door. Usually, when I woke up in the mornings, I would be at my castle, and I would spend at least two minutes trying to figure out which car I wanted to drive for the day. But since

I slept at the nut house, there was only one car to choose, which was the car that I came there in last night. This was my baby. It was my 2019 Cadillac Escalade. I swear I loved this car more than any car that I owned.

I wasn't in a rush to make it to the office, so I figured that I would stop by this morning to visit my ole girl at the shelter. Her shelter was voted the number one shelter in Miami, and over the years, she's won her fair share of awards for it. Because my mother was once a single mother herself and had to take on the task of raising three kids on her own, she was able to empathize with a lot of the women who either came in by themselves or came in with their children. The shelter, of course, offered them a place to stay, helped them sign up for government benefits, helped them set up job interviews, and provided food for them and the kids plus clothing.

All types of people came into the shelter including recovering drug addicts, domestic abuse victims, and just women who had fallen on hard times. My oldest sister, Ocean, was my mom's partner, and over the years had become a great asset.

Ocean was married to my homeboy, Neo. He had businesses just like I did, but his business was more so hookah lounges because that's what was popular in Miami. Ocean didn't necessarily have to work, and Neo made that clear to her all the time, but she made it her duty to come down to the shelter every day and help my ole girl with everything she needed. Neo's ass only wanted my sister home because he was trying to knock her up, but for whatever reason,

Ocean wasn't ready. I didn't know too much about it because I tried to stay out of people's shit, especially when it didn't have a damn thing to do with me. As long as he wasn't disrespecting or putting his hands on my sister, then I was staying out of it.

I quickly pulled my car into the parking lot, and just like every morning, there was a line of women and their children waiting to get inside the shelter. Every time I came there, my stomach turned because once upon a time, I was that boy standing in line with my ole girl and looking at her as if she was the one who had all the answers.

One would think that as much as I came down to help out in whatever way I could, that I would have become used to seeing stuff like this, but I didn't think that I would ever fully accept the fact that it was always MY people struggling. Each time I saw a crying mother standing in line with her children, I swear it felt like I was witnessing this shit for the first time all over again. I hated to come down there driving this expensive ass car while struggling people stood in the line, so I made sure that I parked my car all the way in the back. They wouldn't even see what I got from out of. The only piece of jewelry I wore was a pinky ring.

When I made it to the line of people, I made sure that I spoke to everyone before I went inside. There were hundreds of beds in the room; some were already made up, and some were empty because people were either in the cafeteria having breakfast, some probably left or were just getting ready to start the day. I spoke to all the workers who were in plain sight and headed to the back where my ole girl's office was.

Like I did each time that I came inside, I knocked and just walked in, never giving her a chance to tell me to come in. She was sitting behind the desk staring at the desktop while her glasses rested on her face. I swear my ole girl didn't look like shit she'd been through. She had a gorgeous face except for the cut that was right above her eyebrow, which my sperm donor had left her with after throwing a glass cup at her. She ended up having to get six stitches that night. I hated having to talk about shit like that, but I swear it made her stronger. This lady sitting here before me now didn't take no shit.

Across from her was Ocean, who had papers spread out across my ole girl's desk and was reading something to her before I walked in. They both turned around to look at me.

"There goes my handsome man," my ole girl cooed when I walked into the office.

I swear no one could hype me up or cheer for me the way my ole girl did.

"What's up, Ma? Ya'll saw the line out there this morning? It's wrapped around the corner," I said, walking further into the office and making sure to playfully nudge Ocean on her head before I walked over to my ole girl and hugged her.

"See, you play too much. I just got my braids done last night, and they are too tight for you to be playing like that," Ocean bitched, as she rolled her eyes and whined the whole damn time she talked.

I loved my sister to death, but she was easily the most dramatic female that I had ever met in my life. Swear I didn't understand for the life of me how Neo put up with her shit for all these years.

"We saw the line. We're in here printing out applications now. You heading into work this morning?" my ole girl asked after she stood up from her desk.

"Yes, I just wanted to drop by first and visit my favorite girl," I said, and Ocean released a grunt.

"I heard you went home last night with another slut. You're going to learn, little brother. I swear you're going to learn," Ocean said, scolding a nigga as if she was my mother, instead of my big sister.

It had been like this for years, though. Her ass was always trying to scold a nigga.

"Why my shorties got to be sluts? I like to think of them as beautiful women. Beautiful women with some good ass taste," I said, and my ole girl's hand came crashing against my chest for cursing in her presence.

"Ima stop hanging out with your snitching ass husband. He always running back and telling you shit. I'm sure he was the one who told you that," I said, this time, getting slapped upside my head for cursing.

"Do what you gotta do, Cortez. I hope your dick falls off while you're in the process of doing it too," Ocean spat as she gathered all the papers that were on the desk and put them in a folder.

I laughed at her comment while my mom shot her an evil look, not finding her comment to be hilarious at all.

"Ocean, watch your damn mouth in front of me! You too, Cortez! Ocean, I've been telling you since ya'll were younger to stay out of your brother's business. If he wants to walk around and be a man whore, let him do that. Worry about your relationship with Neo. I have been telling you this for years. Cortez, you leave your sister alone. Ya'll haven't been in this room with each other for more than five minutes, and I'm already breaking up this damn bickering," she said.

Ocean and I had a lot of similar ways. My mom liked to say that she was just me in a dress, and because of that, we tended to butt heads a lot, but it was never serious where we would stop talking to each other or anything like that. Neither of us got the chance to respond to our ole girl because seconds later, the door opened, and it was our little sister, Queen.

My baby sister was eighteen years old, and best believe that she lived up to her name. Her little ass was spoiled as fuck, even though it was me who played a big role in that shit. For her eighteenth birthday, she had the nerve to ask me to get her a Bentley truck, and guess what? My dumb ass got it. Even got it custom made for her too. Queen was a good kid, though. She made good grades in school and had already received over a dozen acceptance letters in the mail for when she starts college in a few months.

I wasn't trying to take the place of a father in her life, but damn, I was just trying to make sure she has love from a man in her life. So, when she gets older and starts dating, she'll never let a nigga do her dirty because she'll know her worth and her damn value. I did shit for her that our bitch ass father was supposed to be doing, and although I couldn't have that title as a father, I liked to think that I was doing a good job with her.

She walked into the room, hugged me, and then she went right for our ole girl. Her spoiled ass wrapped her arms around our mom, and I swear I wanted to walk out of the room and head to work because knowing Queen, this was some damn bullshit. One time, her ass came in the house crying and shit, and she got me all riled up, thinking something was wrong, only for her to be crying because she didn't know what she wanted to wear to the Beyoncé concert. I could have killed her ass that day.

"What's wrong with you, Queen?" my ole girl asked her like she was annoyed.

Everyone knew her ass was drama. My ole girl's voice was literally dripping in, *here we go again with this bullshit!* Although Queen was older now, in her heart, I really believed her little ass felt that she was still a baby and that everyone around her had to cater to her needs because that's the way it was when she was younger. She was usually the one who would get consoled the most and get extra attention.

"I don't want to say it in front of Cortez. I didn't think he was going to be here," she sadly said. She was speaking to my ole girl as if a nigga wasn't even in the room.

"What could you possibly say in front of them that you can't say in front of me? Go ahead. I'm listening," I said, quickly coming out of that cool, big brother mode and going into the big brother that didn't take any shit.

Her eyes landed on mine, and then they went back to our mother's right before she released a sigh. For some reason, I got the feeling that whatever she was getting ready to say, I wasn't going to like it.

"Marcus broke up with me this morning," she said.

Hearing my little sister say some shit like that felt like I'd been shot in the damn chest because I didn't know shit about no fuckin' Marcus. Who the fuck was Marcus? When the fuck did this nigga even come into the picture?

"What? Why?" Ocean jumped in.

It was obvious from her tone that she knew who Marcus was. Hell, from the look on my ole girl's face, I knew she knew this Marcus nigga too.

"Yo, who the fuck is Marcus, and why is it that I'm just now finding out about this nigga? Let me find out that ya'll keeping secrets from me," I growled.

"Boss, please! Not right now. Why did he break up with you?" my ole girl dismissed me and asked Queen.

"Fuck why he broke up with her! He broke up with her because her ass don't need to be having no boyfriend! You're eighteen years old girl, fuck you need a boyfriend for? Your boyfriend should be school, studying, and college applications. Where this nigga from? Where he live? Take me to him right now. I swear I just want to talk." I said everything in one breath because this shit was new to me, and it was something that I didn't want to even accept.

It took me back to my younger years, and it made me

think about the way that niggas I was cool with would dog their shorties at that age. I didn't include myself in that shit because my ass had been tied down since I was nine years old until five years ago when my fiancée died, so with me being tied down, I didn't have time to be out there cheating and shit. Unless a nigga in his teens was truly invested in a girl, a relationship was nothing but a heartbreak that was bound to happen, and I didn't want that for Queen. Niggas are horny at eighteen, and I'd be damned if a lil nigga thought that he was going to be fuckin' on my little sister.

"I swear you remind me of your father sometimes, Cortez! For goodness sake, she's eighteen years old, which to me makes her a mature adult. What she and Marcus have is innocent so you can calm down. He's a good kid, just like Queen is. I've met both of his parents and everything. Marcus isn't like the gangbangers that you were hanging out with when you were her age," my ole girl said.

Truthfully, I'd stopped listening to her the moment she compared me to that fuck nigga.

"Don't compare me to that man because he and I don't have shit in common!" I spat.

"Ocean and Queen, go outside, so I can talk to your brother," my ole girl said, and best believe she didn't have to say it twice.

My ole girl played with us a lot, but we knew when she was serious. Even now as a grown ass man, I'd never get so comfortable with myself that I felt like I could disrespect the woman who had brought my ass into this world. The same woman who had sacrificed so much shit for myself and my siblings growing up. So, best believe if she had told me to get out too, I would have left as well. When Ocean and Queen were out of the room, she walked over to me and placed one of her hands on my shoulder.

"Cortez, you hate him just as much as I do. I don't make it a habit of comparing you two because, quite frankly, you are more of a man than he will ever be. Sometimes, when you say little shit, you just remind me of him because even you know how controlling his ass used to be. You know our relationship was more of a dictatorship than a real relationship. You may not want to accept it, but baby, sometimes your ass can be a little controlling.

"I know you mean well when it comes to Queen, but she is not that same little girl that you used to get into the bed with at night and read her bedtime stories before she fell asleep. Just like when you were fourteen and reality hit me that you weren't a baby anymore, that's the same thing happening right now with your sister. In your defense, we should have told you, but you reacted the same way that we knew you would react when you found out about Marcus, which is why we thought that it would be best if we had kept it a secret from you. Lighten up on her, Cortez," my ole girl said right before she kissed my cheek.

"How old that nigga is, Ma?" was all I asked, and she laughed.

"He's eighteen, just like Queen is. You'll like him, Boss," she said, and I quickly shook my head.

"No, the hell I won't. Queen is still a baby in my eyes, so any little nigga who finds himself attracted to my sister and all that other bullshit that comes with being in a relationship, hell no, I'm not going to like him," I told her.

She rolled her eyes at me as she waved the conversation off.

"Ocean was right about what she said to you earlier. You not tired of going home with hoes?" my ole girl asked.

I released a sigh. Had I known that I was going to bring my ass down there this morning and get lectured, I would have just taken my black ass into the office. Usually, my ole girl tried to stay out of a nigga's personal life, but when she did, she would constantly push the issue. The shit was fuckin' annoying. She knew me better than anybody else in this fuckin' world, so she knew that all of these hoes that I was fuckin' and catching no feelings for them in the process was just an escape mechanism for me.

Visions of seeing my fiancée that night when I had to come down to the hospital and claim the body was still in my head. I could still feel that cold ass room, and I know this may sound a little bizarre, but every once in a while, I could still smell the scent in that room. It smelled like death; hard, cold, miserable death. The image of that single bullet hole in her head, and when I moved the paper blanket over her body and saw the bullet holes in her stomach still registered in my mind. I still remember the doctor walking over to me, putting his hand on my shoulder, and telling me that my fiancée and my daughter had both died. So, excuse me if I fucked a few hoes from time to time to run away from my problems. I smoked weed too at night to ease my pain, but that was it.

I wasn't saying that I was perfect, but I was coping in a way that was better than how most people would have been dealing with something like this. I wasn't abusing drugs, nor was I abusing alcohol. I fucked, smoked, and I kept all this shit bottled inside of me, so I wasn't a threat to anyone nor myself.

"Ma, you know as well as I know that I don't take these hoes to my house. Look, I'm chilling. I'm wrapping up my jimmy, so you don't have to worry about me catching no diseases or making you a grandmother with no woman that I'm not serious about. In all seriousness, I'm not looking for nobody. My businesses are the only things that I have interest in and the only thing that's really worth loving in my life," I told her.

"Who the hell said you had to go out and look for her, son? What if God already has her waiting for you, and He's just waiting for the perfect opportunity to place her in your life? I know your businesses are doing great, and you're very wealthy and all of that, but at the end of a long workday, son, you go home by yourself. You live in that beautiful, seven bedroom home by yourself, and although you won't admit it to me, I know that it has to get lonely in there.

"I'm your mother, and Lord knows that I hate to see you hurting, but Cortez, Amari isn't coming back. I loved that girl like I birthed her, and I wanted nothing more than for the two of you to get married and bless me with some beautiful, black grandbabies, but we all lost that opportunity the day she was murdered. Although we don't want to, we have to accept it and move on. We can still love her because God knows that I do, and I can only imagine the type of love that you have for her. I know Amari wouldn't have wanted to see you like this. She would want you to be happy, Boss. Ask yourself are you happy," she said.

I swear she touched on a lot of shit.

"If I leave out of the office at a reasonable time, I'll come over tonight for dinner. Love you, Ma," I quickly said right before I leaned in and kissed her on her cheek. And just like that, I was running. Running away from all problems. Running away from those things of the world that would cause me pain.

CHAPTER FOUR

Do you know that I arrived at the church this morning where the funeral was being held, only to be turned around with my kids because of the simple fact that our names weren't on the list? The list! Who has a fuckin' list for a damn funeral? Crazy thing is, no one ever told me where the funeral would even be held today. You'd be surprised at the extreme measures that I had to go to this morning just to find out where the funeral was taking place.

At exactly 6:00 a.m., I woke up in a hotel room with my children and I began to get myself ready. Let me backtrack a little bit and tell you all why it's been a week and two days that I've been staying in a hotel room, and why my children and I were living out of a duffle bag. The night I found out that the man I'd spent the last four years of my life with was actually married, I came back home from the hospital to some bullshit.

Every single photo frame in the house that held pictures of our children and me was gone. Any proof that I needed to show his wife that Dewayne was my fiancé was gone! I'm talking about social security cards, birth certificates, just anything that I could use to back up everything that I was saying was gone. The shit scared the fuck out of me because I didn't know who had done this. It had to have been the same person who'd deleted all the pictures and videos from my phone.

I felt like someone was playing a sick joke on me, so that night, I packed up as much as the kids and my stuff as I possibly could, and I got the fuck out of dodge. I didn't want to stick around and find out who was playing this sick ass joke on me. That night, I had to have called Juju's phone over one thousand times before she blocked me because something told me that she had to have known what the hell was going on.

For nine fuckin' days, I've been trying to piece this shit together. I've been cursing my own self out, asking myself how the hell could I have been so stupid to the point that I let this man come into my life and tell me anything. Was I that fuckin' naïve? Was I that stupid to actually believe that a man like Dewayne was only in association with Juju as a family member? Why the hell didn't I push the issue when he told me that he'd cut his family off? Why didn't I ask him to elaborate more when he told me that bullshit four years ago?

Then, there was his wife. A wife who had birthed four children for him, while my placenta hadn't even been pushed out of me yet, and he was already telling me to tell the doctor that I wanted my tubes tied. What the fuck was wrong with me?

After nine days of thinking about this shit, I was still left at square one. I could literally come up with nothing that would explain why Dewayne would play me like this. I couldn't come up with nothing on why he would do our children like this. I was just waiting for someone to come and tell me that it was a prank because this is what it felt like. If this happened to be real life and the characters from this bullshit were actually real life people, then I hated Dewayne. I hated him for doing our children like this. I hated him for thinking that my heart was a toy and that he could just play with it until he got tired.

I had been crying for days because I actually believed this man when he would tell me that he would be out of town for business. Seems to me like whenever he would tell me that lie, he would actually be home with this family; his real family for that matter.

After days of coming up short, I woke up this morning with a purpose. Once I was dressed and had the kids dressed, I drove us to Juju's house. For three fuckin' hours, I waited in the car with my children until she came out dressed in her funeral attire. The moment she backed out of her driveway, I followed her. I followed her for forty-five minutes until she pulled the car up to a church which had to have housed hundreds of vehicles in the parking lot.

I waited about ten minutes before I got out of the car. Once I did, I grabbed each of my children's hands, and the three of us made our way to the church doors, only to be met by security who turned the three of us around when it came up that none of our kids' names were on the list. Not even his fuckin' children's names were on the list to attend their own's father's funeral.

As much as I wanted to stand there and cry, I felt like these past few days, I had already done too much in front of my children, so I didn't. Like a mother who felt like she had the weight of the world on her shoulders, I grabbed both of the kids' hands again and turned around. Again, we sat in the car for almost three hours, just waiting for the services to be over.

The moment we saw the pallbearers walking out of the church holding onto the beautiful, gold casket was when I sat up in my seat because I knew then that the funeral was over. I had visions of myself running up to the pallbearers, opening the casket, and slapping and spitting on Dewayne for doing this shit to me, but I remained in my car. I watched as his body was placed in the back of a fancy limousine, and after that, folks started spilling out of the church like sardines.

A wave of sadness fell over me when I saw his wife. Her three children were right by her side, and she was carrying their baby boy in her hands. There were big, oversized frames on her face, which took up the majority of it so I couldn't tell if she was crying or not, but more than likely she was. I watched a number of people walk up to her and speak. Some gave hugs, so I knew that they were more than likely sending her their condolences. I couldn't help but think, what about us? What about myself and my kids? We were hurt just as badly. We lost someone too.

Although it turned out that he was just a piece of lying shit, it didn't take away from the hurt we were feeling. Lord knows I didn't want to accept it, but I felt like I was just the sideline after all.

"Mommy, when are we leaving? I'm starvinnggg," Storm whined from the backseat of the car.

I'd packed them a bag filled with snacks and drinks, but we'd spent a total of almost six hours in the car today, so they'd finished all of the snacks like thirty minutes ago. I had them entertained by watching *Boss Baby* on the screens that were on the back of my chair and the passenger chair, but I knew that it was only so many times that they could watch that movie before they started whining.

"Soon, baby. I promise, just one more stop, and then I'll take you all to wherever you want to eat," I let them know.

"Yayyy," they both cooed.

After another fifteen minutes, the limousine finally left the church parking lot, and what did I choose to do? I followed it. They could turn my children and me around at the church all they wanted, but the gravesite was public property, so I dared them to try and turn me around there. It was about a ten-minute drive to the gravesite, and I blended right on in with the rest of the friends and family who were on their way as police stopped traffic so we could get there in a timely manner.

Once my car was parked on the grass, like everyone else, I finally got out with my children. I broke it down to my children the night we got to the hotel after leaving the hospital and tried to explain death to three-year-olds the best way I knew how, but I didn't think that they understood it just yet. I let them know that their daddy wouldn't be coming back, and neither of them batted an eye. They say that children could always see the bad in people, so the fact that my kids didn't show an ounce of emotion once I announced that Dewayne was gone had spoken volumes to me.

There were a lot of people at the gravesite waiting to see Dewayne's body lowered into the ground and witness the final goodbyes. I stood with my sunglasses on to conceal the bags that were under my eyes due to me not getting any sleep and to cover the pain because I didn't want weakness to show. These days, I felt like weak is exactly what I was. I stayed in the back with my children as they asked me a million times what was going on. The service was short, and soon enough, people were dropping their single roses on top of the casket. Then just like that, they headed back to their cars.

No one spoke to me as they walked past my children and me because no one knew me. I was waiting for Juju to walk past because I had words for her. It went from hundreds of people standing out here to maybe fifty just standing around. I was beginning to think that Juju had left already, and I just didn't see her, but all of a sudden, I heard her voice, and I turned to where it was coming from. She was squatting down and saying something to one of the wife's children. I watched her wipe their eyes and say something to them. Although I tried to read her lips, I failed miserably. I always felt like Juju was a bad person, but this just further reminded me that I was right this whole time.

"Auntie Juju!" Storm screamed.

I tried to quickly place my hand over her mouth, but it was too late. Juju had already looked along with the wife and their kids. I didn't want things to go down like this, but I wouldn't scold my daughter because she was innocent in this entire thing and didn't know. It wasn't her fault that she didn't know her auntie wasn't shit. Although Juju was technically her cousin, my kids always called her Auntie Juju.

I saw words exchanged between Juju and the wife, and before I knew it, the two of them were walking over in my direction. The wife was empty-handed, meaning she was holding the baby. They walked with purpose, especially the wife. I had never fought a day in my life, but I promise that I was on whatever they were on! They couldn't even begin to feel my pain so I may have the strength of a damn giant in me right now.

Once they were close enough, I pulled my kids from in front of me and placed them behind me.

"At my husband's funeral? You're really going to do this disrespectful shit at my husband's funeral? What type of woman do you call herself? Where the hell is your pride? On top of that, you bring your two children down here to witness you act a monkey! A week ago, you caught me at my lowest, so as much as I wanted to beat your ass, I couldn't because I didn't have the damn strength. I just went nine days without the man that I've spent years with, and you can't even begin to feel what I'm feeling, so if I were you, I would walk away, and I would do it fast before I kill you! I swear to God that I will kill you!" she screamed, and her voice cracked.

"Camila, calm down! The kids aren't that far away, and they are probably listening to you. Let's just go," Juju tried to reason as she placed her hand on her shoulder and tried to walk her away, but I interrupted her whole little plan that she was trying to concoct right in front of us.

"We both know that the only reason you are trying to get her to walk away is so that your part in all of this won't come to light. I've always thought that you were shady, Juju, but I would have never thought that you were this low down and dirty. To literally stand your ass here and to pretend that you don't know me is one thing, but to pretend that you don't know my kids is another.

"These are kids who spent the night at your house whenever Dewayne and I would go out. How dare you pretend not to know them when you fuckin' begged me to let you be the godmother to them when you found out that I was pregnant, but I said no! Camila, I don't know you, and you don't know me, but just know that I don't gain shit from doing this! You think I want to do this shit in front of my children?

"I may not be the prettiest woman in the world, and I

may not have the best looking body, but you have to believe me when I say that I've spent the last four years of my life with your husband! I have no proof, but if I have to go to the moon and back, I will prove to you that the man you were married to wasn't as clean as you thought he was," I let her know.

"You cannot tell me a damn thing when it comes to my husband! I made the list of everyone who could be allowed into the funeral, and side chick and oops babies were nowhere on the list. I have power, control, and a reach out of this world so I will make sure that you and your kids suffer from this. You all will not eat another dime off my husband. In a blink of an eye or with one phone call, I can have the three of you put off this fuckin' Earth, so if I were you, I would leave this situation alone.

"Dewayne had one woman in this life, which is me, Camila. He has four children, whose names are Christiana, Crystal, Dewayne Jr, and our new baby boy, Christopher. As you can see, you all don't fit in the picture. My husband is dead, so what the hell are you even looking for? Why do you keep following me around? If you're after me for some money, I suggest you find yourself the nearest food stamp line because you will not get a hand out from me," she nastily spat.

"I guess he left himself behind two juniors then because our son is named Dewayne Jr as well. When all of this dies down, you'll realize that your husband was just as low down and dirty as his cousin standing right here," I said.

I had to do something before I left, so I pulled my fist

back and punched the shit out of Juju. That punch was long overdue and had my kids not been with me, I swear I would have done more. I heard her crying and screaming at the top of her lungs, but I was already walking back to the car with the kids, so all the noise that she was making just faded off into the distance.

CHAPTER FIVE

"Juju, come here," I peeked out of my bedroom and called out.

The funeral was now over, and all four of my children were resting. Juju was out front cleaning up the kitchen after the last of my husband's family had left. Being around a bunch of people was literally the last thing that I wanted to be doing right now, but Dewayne's family insisted, so I allowed them to have the repast at my home.

The past few days had been sort of a blur to me. If it weren't for my children, I knew for a fact that I would have checked out a long time ago because I was hurting deeply. The man who had been in my life ever since I was nineteen years old was taken from me, and I didn't know how to deal with it. It just didn't seem real, you know? I like to think that the ones around me are immune from certain things happening to them. A car accident, really? Dewayne was literally one of the safest drivers that I knew. He was one of those drivers who wouldn't start his car until everyone had on their seatbelt.

I always felt safe in the car with him because he would always take the proper safety precautions. I guess I never really thought about the fact that an accident could happen without him being the one to have caused it. Sadly, when we got the full details on the crash, we were told that a drunk driver running a red light had slammed his car directly into Dewayne's and ended my husband's life in seconds. By the time I was informed of what happened, Dewayne was already at the hospital. Once I arrived at the hospital with my family along with his, we were given the devasting news that he was dead.

My heart couldn't stand to have seen him in the condition that he was in once the doctor told us his injuries. We were told that his neck was broken, and you could literally see the bones sticking out of it along with other gruesome things, and we all agreed that we didn't want to see him in that state. We all wanted to remember Dewayne in the perfect physical condition that we had all last seen him in.

The last image I had of my husband was before he'd gone out at night. Sad thing is, I can't even tell you where he was taking off to. He never told me his destination, nor did he let me know how long he would be gone. He just simply told me not to wait up for him and to make sure that I locked up, and I'd done both things. Had I known that would be the last time I saw my husband, I would have kissed him longer than I'd done and told him I loved him a few more times, so that when he died, there would literally be zero doubt about the feelings that I had invested in him.

Our baby boy, Christopher, only got to spend three days with Dewayne because three days after his birth, my husband was back on the road for work. He'd literally just gotten back home the day before the car accident. Everything was perfect when we came home. He surprised me with flowers, my favorite chocolate, and he even handed me a card with plane tickets to Paris for next month to celebrate my thirty-first birthday.

If I weren't still sore from just giving birth, and if I weren't still bleeding, we would have made love that night. Instead, we just cuddled with each other as he held me tight and told me over one hundred times how much he loved me. It felt good to have that because I'll admit that our relationship had been a little rocky for years now.

My husband was a workaholic, and I was a 'momaholic,' always in mom mode with the children and feeling like I never got a break. There was no middle ground in our relationship because he was always working while I was always mothering. That took a toll on the marriage, and it caused me to complain a lot because, at the end of the day, all I really wanted was my husband home with me.

Although there were problems and disputes along with disagreements here and there, that's all it was. It wasn't anything more than me feeling like I wanted to have my husband home with me more, so I didn't know how the hell this woman was claiming to be engaged to my husband, let alone have kids by him, who by the way, didn't look shit like Dewayne. Those kids of hers were every bit of her, and I didn't see a lick of Dewayne in them. She wasn't even my husband's type!

I was a Hispanic woman, and my husband told me that he's always dated Hispanic women. Yes, he was a black man, but he told me that he never dated his kind, which was how I knew for a fact that this woman was lying. Plus, she was fat. I mean, she wasn't sloppily built or anything like that, but she was a thicker woman, and everyone who knew Dewayne knew that he preferred his woman to be petite.

What the hell was up with her skin too? I didn't notice it the first time I saw her because I was so angry at the accusations that she was throwing out, but I damn sure noticed it today at the gravesite. It was all on her hands, above her eye, and everything. Again, all those physical traits were things that I knew my husband wouldn't have been attracted to. I'll admit that she was beautiful, but that was the only thing. A pretty face was only worth so much.

"Hey, the kitchen is clean. I was getting ready to head out now," Juju said, walking in the bedroom and taking a seat at the foot of the bed.

Her left eye was swollen and damn near shut from the punch that was delivered to her a few hours ago. Honestly, I didn't know if I felt bad for her or not. I didn't know because although I said that there is no way in hell that my husband would have stepped out on our marriage with that woman, it was something about the pain and the seriousness in the woman's eyes that had me on the fence with my feelings. I could go on and on about my husband having a type, but like the woman said, what was she looking to gain?

Every time I felt myself beginning to believe her, I would think about the fact that she had no proof to back up anything that she was saying. Where were the pictures? Where were the birth certificates with my husband's signature? She literally had nothing. Then, when I would stop believing everything she was said, I would think back to the night at the hospital in the family waiting room.

She said personal things about my husband that only someone who was close with him would know. She knew Dewayne's shoe size, the foods he was allergic to, which hand he wrote with; all of the things that you would know from being close with him. I didn't want her to feel as if I believed anything that she said, which was why my approach was so strong with her, but in the back of my mind, of course, I took everything into consideration that she'd said to me.

"Juliana, you and I have been close friends for just as long as I've been with Dewayne. I look at you as a little sister. I have shared some of my deepest secrets with you, I never lied to you, and I trust you, but I don't know how to feel about this. Right now, it's just me and you in this room. I want you to look me in my eyes and tell me that everything that this woman said is a complete fabrication. I want you to tell me the truth! If you know her, say that! If you were a part of whatever the hell my husband had with her, please tell me. This is my life we're talking about. I want to know if I'm mourning the death of the man that I was deeply in love with, or if I'm mourning the death of a man that I barely even knew," I said in all seriousness with my hands folded across my chest as I stood in front of her with my eyes directly on hers.

She fumbled with her hands for a few seconds, and then she finally released a sigh.

"I'll tell you the truth. On everything I love, I swear I barely know that woman. She and I go to the same hair salon, and word goes around Miami fast, so she knew that Dewayne was my cousin. It just so happened that every time I would go to the salon to get my hair done, she would be there as well. She used to beg me to set her up on a date with him. I remember one time she told me that she would pay for my hair if I gave Dewayne her number, but I refused, because like I kept telling her, he was married.

"The same way she just keeps popping up on you with those kids is the way she does me. I feel as though she uses those kids as a pawn so that people will have sympathy for her. When I met her, she already had the kids, so I know for a fact that those babies aren't my cousins. Why are you even entertaining her? You said it yourself that you know that she isn't Dewayne's type," she said.

"The pain in her eyes, Juju! That's why I'm entertaining it! Her kids called you Auntie Juju with confidence! That wasn't just something that they'd said for the first time! If she was making this whole thing up, why the hell would she string her kids along in all of this? Most importantly, how the hell did she know to come to the hospital the night of the accident? She came looking specifically for you! She called you Juliana, and we all know that only people who are close with you call you Juliana. You didn't correct her when she called you by your first name. If you are hiding something from me, Juju, tell me now, or I swear on my children that I will never forgive you for this. I promise you I won't!" I screamed, probably the loudest that I'd ever screamed at anyone in my entire life because I was so serious about this.

"Camila, I promise you that I don't know that lady. She knows me by Juliana because the hair stylist that we both go to calls me Juliana, so she started saying it from there. That girl is fuckin' crazy, and deep down in her heart, she truly believes that she and I are the best of friends. Although I don't have children of my own, you know that I love kids. One day at the shop, the kids were there, and I promise you she had them calling me Auntie Juju out of nowhere. I didn't want to be mean to the kids, so I let them call me that.

"Listen, I have no idea how the hell she knew to come to the hospital that night because I didn't call her. I don't even have her damn number. The only thing that I know about her is that her name is Winter, she has two children, and that we go to the same place to get our hair done. Oh, and that she's fuckin' crazy! That's it, Camila. I promise you," Juju said, looking me dead in my eyes.

"Let me see your phone," I said.

Juju rolled her eyes, and without hesitation, she stood up from the bed and walked out of the room to more than likely retrieve her phone from her purse or something. Because I didn't want her to have time to delete anything, I followed behind her. Her purse was on the kitchen table, and I watched as she dug inside and found her iPhone X. I stood over her as she used her finger to unlock the phone, and as soon as she did that, I snatched it from her hands.

She mentioned that the woman's name was Winter, so I scrolled through her contacts for that name, but I didn't find it. Next, I went through her call log and scrolled all the way down to last week to see if she was in contact with a number the night that we were all at the hospital. I wanted to know if it was she who placed the call for Winter to have known to come down to the hospital and look for my husband. Again, there was nothing. Just conversations from her family and some of her friends that I knew.

Juliana had over 1,000 pictures and videos in her phone, and I stood there checking everything. I even went through her social media accounts to see what she posted. I didn't have social media; therefore I didn't always see the things that Juliana posted. I checked her emails, voicemails, and even went through her trash in her email to see if she'd deleted anything, but there was nothing. After about twenty minutes of searching her phone and coming up with nothing, I handed her the phone back and took a seat at the kitchen table, placing my hand over my head because I was just so lost.

"If I knew more about this situation, I swear that I would have told you, Camila, but I don't. Look who you're married to. Damn near everyone knows your husband. Therefore, they know that he has a lot of money. This is just a bitch with her hand out, looking to make a come up off you. You have to be strong when it comes to shit like this. With Dewayne dead, I'm pretty sure that all types of bitches are about to start popping out of the bushes claiming to have a baby by him because they're looking for money. They're looking to destroy his image, and most importantly, they're looking to get under your skin. You can't let that happen," Juju warned me.

I let everything that she said sink in for a little bit.

"I'm going to head to Columbia this weekend for a few months to be with my family. I don't have the strength these days to juggle four kids on my own. Plus, I want to get out of this house because it's depressing me. Every day that I'm here, it reminds me of what I had with Dewayne and what I'll never get back. I can't stand to sleep in that bed because it smells just like him. I'm not sure how long I'm going to be gone, but hopefully, when I come back, I'll be stronger," I said.

She nodded her head while she walked over and wrapped her arms around me, giving me a hug that I so desperately needed.

"It's going to be alright, Camila. Just know that if you need me for anything, I'm here," she assured me, and that was that.

I didn't necessarily know if I felt better now that she and I had had this conversation, but I will say that I felt a little bit more at ease. When I was a little girl, and I would sneak and do stuff, my mom would always preach to me that whatever I was doing in the dark would eventually come to light. If this woman had dealings with my husband after all, and those were his children for sure, then it would one day be brought to light. If she was some crazy person who was trying to pin babies on my husband and looking for a handout like Juju said she was, then that would come to light too. Right now, I wasn't thinking about it. I just needed to be strong for my children and somehow find a way to be even stronger for myself.

CHAPTER SIX

"Don't play with your food, Mommy," my three-year-old son said, knocking me out of the daydream that I was in.

I had the fork in the mashed potatoes that I'd ordered, and I was stirring them around because I didn't have an appetite. Food was literally the last thing on my mind these days. The funeral was now over along with the repast, and as promised, I'd let the kids pick where they wanted to go for lunch. It was no surprise that they'd both picked Texas Roadhouse. My kids loved coming there simply for the bread.

For the hour that we'd been here, it had mainly just been the two of them talking amongst each other because I was in a daze. I wasn't myself these days. Quite frankly, I was somewhat in denial because I was still calling Dewayne's phone with hopes of him answering so he could explain this entire thing to me because it just wasn't making any sense. As much as I wanted to hate him, I just needed answers. I needed to know why this had to happen to me.

If he had such a beautiful family, then why did he have to come and string me along? These were all things that I so desperately needed answers to. Sad part about it is I knew that I would never get these answers. I couldn't talk to his wife because she wouldn't even stop to hear me out for a second, and I didn't want to talk to Juju anymore. If I were to be around that bitch, I swear I would have killed her. That punch that I'd just given her was the least of what I really wanted to do.

"I'm going to save the rest of it for later, baby. Are ya'll full?" I asked the twins.

My kids were such messy eaters, and even with the napkins that I'd placed on their shirts, they still managed to somehow have ketchup and mustard all on their hands, faces, and shirt from the chicken tenders and fries that they'd eaten. I removed myself from the booth that I was sitting in and joined them as I reached into the bookbag that I brought with me and pulled out some wipes. I wiped both of their hands and their faces, and in seconds, they looked clean again.

"Yes, we're full, Mommy," they both said.

At the same time, the waitress came over and handed me

the check for our meal. I quickly dug into my purse, found my wallet, and passed her my debit card.

With a smile on her face, she took the card and skipped off while I used the to-go box that she'd given me to pack up my food. I had barely even touched my food. All I did was take a few sips from the water that I'd ordered. In just a few seconds, I noticed that our waitress was heading back our way. It was way too quick for her to have checked us out already. I tried to read the look on her face, and honestly, it was hard to decipher.

"Ma'am, would you happen to have a different form of payment? The card was declined. I ran it three times," she told me.

"That's impossible. I know for a fact that I have money on that card," I said, my voice holding much confidence because I knew that there was plenty of money on that account.

"I'll give you a minute, and then I'll come back," she said and dropped the card along with the check on the table.

I pulled my phone out of my purse and quickly went to the Bank of America app to see how much money was in my account. Something definitely had to be wrong with their system because there was always money on this card. Although I didn't work because Dewayne was the bread-winner, he made sure to keep my account loaded.

In a few short seconds, I had the app up, and I could have died when I saw that the balance in the account was 0.01. I literally had one cent in my checking account after having a balance of over $20,000 just yesterday. There was almost fifty grand in my savings account, and that had been wiped away as well. My hands started shaking and sweat formed on my forehead because it just wasn't making any sense. I checked the account activity and saw that the money that was removed from my account was processed early this morning.

"How can this happen?" I mumbled.

The only people who had access to my account was Dewayne and me. This was the only form of payment that I had on me. A lightbulb went off in my head when I realized that I had two twenty-dollar bills in my wallet. I could see our waitress looking at me from across the room, so I waved for her to come over, and I handed her the cash.

I felt so bad when she came back with the change, and I didn't leave a tip. I didn't know if the change that I got back was going to be the last bit of money that I had to my name so I couldn't take the risk of leaving it for her, and it left me with less than I already had. The twins were asking a million questions and wanting to know what was going on, but I couldn't answer them right now because even I didn't know what was going on.

Back inside the car

"What do you mean there is nothing that you can do? Money just magically disappears from my account, and there isn't a damn thing that you can do? Are you serious right now?" I screamed to the customer service representative at Bank of America over the phone, as I tried to figure out what was going on with my account.

"Ma'am, like I've been telling you for the past ten minutes, you are not an authorized user on the account, so I cannot share that information with you. Unless you are Dewayne Stewart, there is nothing that I can share with you because it's his account. Not only is that an issue, but you also don't know the verbal password, so I can't help you with this matter. Let's put it like this. This account, ending in 4576 belongs to Dewayne Stewart. If you were the one spending the money and things like that, then think of it as the user just allowing you to borrow the card, because, at the end of the day, it was his funds. It's his account, ma'am. You said your name was Winter Rivera, correct? That name shows nowhere on the account, ma'am. In fact, your name isn't even the name listed on the card. You have to get in contact with Mr. Stewart to resolve this issue," he said.

"I can't get in contact with Mr. Stewart because he's dead!" I screamed, and then I ended the phone call.

I was beginning to lose my fuckin' mind. I literally had $10.67 to my name, and that was nowhere near enough money to accommodate myself and my children.

"What's wrong, Mommy?" Storm asked me from the backseat.

"Storm, not right now! Please, not right now! Just give Mommy a second, okay?" I yelled at her.

From the look on her face, I could tell that I'd hurt her feelings. I couldn't console her right now because I needed to figure out what was going on. My gas light had just come on, which made me suck my teeth. I wanted to scream to the top of my lungs, but I didn't want to scare the children. We were fifteen minutes away from the house, and the whole drive over, I had the music off. I just needed my thoughts at this moment. The kids weren't even talking amongst themselves.

I finally made it to the gated community that I lived in, and I used the fob that I had to let myself in. As I got closer to my home, I saw a big *America Moving & Packaging* van. I thought nothing of it because this was a newly built community, so people were moving there all the time. It wasn't until I saw that the truck was parked in our driveway that I raised my eyebrows.

"What the fuck is going on?" I mumbled to myself.

Like a drunk driver, I pulled the car on the grass in front of my house and put the car in park. I watched as two movers came out of the house carrying the beautiful Sofia Vergara living room set that I had just purchased about a month ago and placed it in the moving truck. Next, two more movers came out hauling the big, 85-inch television that was in the den area. After them, I saw a white man dressed in a nice, army green three-piece suit with a clipboard in his hands.

"Wait right here. Neither of you get of out of this car. Do you hear me?" I yelled at the twins, and they both nodded.

I quickly got out of the car and slammed the door, making sure that I locked it. With the speed of a cheetah, I sprinted over to the front door demanding to know what the hell was going on.

"What the hell are you doing? Who are you? Why are they just taking my things out of here like this? Can you put my fuckin' couch down!" I yelled at the movers, but my words fell on deaf ears as they continued to do their job.

The white man who was dressed to the nines in his suit stopped talking to one of the movers and walked over to me. He had a look of annoyance on his face as he looked me up and down and made his way over to me.

"Excuse me, ma'am, but are you lost?" he asked.

I'd never really been attracted to white men before, but he was beautiful. He had like a country, southern slang when he talked, which I also found attractive. He had a pale skin tone with the most beautiful set of blue eyes that I'd ever seen in my life. His hair was like a honey blonde color, and before he even reached me, I could smell the intoxicating scent of his cologne. Although he was attractive as hell, it was something about his presence that screamed he wasn't a good person. I could tell by the way he looked at me. He stared at me as if I was the dirt on the bottom of his very expensive Christian Louboutin shoes.

I left home for a few days, and the moment I came back, people were moving out all of my things, like this shit was okay.

"No, I'm not lost! I live here with my fiancé and our two children! What the hell are they doing? For the past week or so, I've been staying in a hotel. I come back, and this is happening! Would you be able to explain this shit to me somehow? Is this the same company that came in here a few days ago and stole the pictures of my fiancé and our children along with birth certificates and copies of social security cards? Somebody better tell me something before I call the fuckin' police! This is burglary!" I screamed.

He sized me up and down again, mumbled something incoherent, and shook his head at me.

"If I wasn't in a professional business, I swear I would want whatever drug you're on for you to even believe for a second that this house belongs to you. This is my client, Dewayne Stewart's home. I'm his lawyer, and not that I have to share any of this with you, but he left it in his will for me to sell this home and give all proceeds to his wife, Camila Stewart. I've been Mr. Stewart's lawyer for almost fifteen years, and I've never heard of you or even seen you for that matter. Who are you again?" he rudely asked me.

"Winter Rivera. I'm his fiancée," I said with the last of the pride that I had left, and he laughed right in my face.

"Fiancée, huh? That's cute. Listen, your name was nowhere in the will, Winter Rivera. Outside of the business relationship that I had with Mr. Stewart, he and I are very close friends so I can assure you right now that you are lying. Even if he did have a fling on the side, he would have told me, and you were never mentioned. If I were you, I would get back into that pretty little car of yours and go home, wherever the hell that is, before you force me to call the police on you for trespassing. You are not an owner of this home, nor is your name anywhere listed on the property so I can have you in handcuffs in seconds if you try me. I don't want to be an asshole because I see two adorable children in the backseat of your car, and I would hate for them to have to witness their mother get arrested right in front of them. Tell me what you want to do, Winter. It's your choice," he said.

He was so heartless about it. I was trying so hard not to cry, but I eventually broke down. I lost it. I crumbled right in front of him, dropping down to my knees as I released a gut-wrenching cry.

"I spent the last two years of my life in this house. Those are me and Dewayne's kids in that backseat. What am I supposed to tell them? Where am I supposed to go?" I cried, not talking to anyone in particular.

He walked over and bent down before me. I used my hands to wipe the tears that had fallen from my eyes and looked up at him. I thought he was going to help me up, but he didn't.

He put his mouth to my ear and whispered, "Honestly, I don't give two fucks about you and those black ass kids. Ya'll can sleep in a fuckin' alley for all that I care. You literally have one second to get your ass up and leave this property. I have six big, strong men in that house who wouldn't mind picking you up from your arms to your legs and throwing your ass out of here. Either way it goes, I bet I have you out of here," he spat, and I quickly got up.

I hightailed it back to the car, and once I was inside, I threw my head back on the headrest in defeat. I literally only had one place that I could go to, which wasn't much of an option because when I left years ago, I was told that I couldn't come back. Trust me, I didn't want to go back, but I didn't have much of a choice. Plus, there were kids involved, so I had to make a decision based on what was good for them and their needs instead of what I wanted. My sister was still in the Navy, so there was no way that I could look to her for help. I didn't want to go to Sandra's house, but it seemed that I didn't have any other option.

I hated to say this, but I was stupid. I let Dewayne make me stupid. I was so wrapped up in feeling like I was so lucky to be with him, that I didn't even realize the danger that I was putting myself and my children in. My name was literally on nothing! Not the house, the cards, nothing! My name wasn't even on this fuckin' car, so I knew that it was only a matter of time before they started looking for it. I never thought to plan smart because I never thought that Dewayne would leave us high and dry like this.

When he was giving me money, the smart thing would've been to open an account that he didn't know about and transfer funds to that account to have on a rainy day like this. At twenty-nine years old, not only was I about to struggle again, but I had to go through the shit with my children.

CHAPTER SEVEN

"Where are we, Mommy? I'm sleepy," my daughter whined from the back seat.

It was going on ten at night, and I was finally pulling my car into a place that I didn't think I would ever have to visit again. I used the last ten dollar bill that I had on me to put gas in my car. For two hours straight, I rode around Miami, and then I ended up parking the car in a parking lot of a plaza as I had another breakdown. I used that time to think about where I would go tonight.

Voices in my head were telling me to go to Sandra's because, at the end of the day, I was still her child. I didn't think that she would be that heartless to turn me away along with her grandchildren. Grandchildren that she had never even met. Then, on the opposing side, I had voices telling me that Sandra's house shouldn't even be an option of places for me to go because of the simple fact that she probably hadn't even changed. She was more than likely still that same mean, hurtful woman that she was when I was a little girl. With all the voices that were speaking to me, I had to act fast because I had my kids out late, and they'd pretty much been inside this car all day.

They didn't deserve for any of this shit to be happening to them. At a time like this, they were supposed to be in their beds, wrapped up, and having a peaceful sleep. Because I knew that I needed to get my kids somewhere with a roof over their head and hopefully in a bed to sleep in, I went against my better judgment and hauled the three of us to Sandra's house.

I'd never been so scared in my life because what happens if she says that we couldn't stay? Where do I go from there? Where do I take my children? Those questions literally scared the shit out of me, and when I was forced to think about it, it forced me to cry some more, simply because I didn't have the answers to any of those questions at the moment.

I hadn't seen Sandra or spoken to her since the day I left. I had years' worth of time to come and make it right with her, but I had gotten so caught up in the relationship that I had with Dewayne that I never thought to do that. As scared as I was, I still shut the car off and released a sigh. All I had were the clothes on my back along with one pair of pajamas in my duffle bag and about four more outfits, some underwear, bras, and a few toiletries. My kids had about a week's worth of pajamas and clothes, and that was it.

"This is my mom's house, your grandmother. Come on," I said, opening the door and helping Storm out of her car seat.

I did the same thing with my son, and soon, the three of us were out of the car. I didn't bother to bring the duffle bag because I didn't know if she was going to let us stay or not. I opened the metal gate and walked up the driveway with my kids. Suddenly, the visions began to come back to me. They were bad visions too. Shit that I didn't want to relive.

Everything about this place was the same. That same ole wooden chair that had been on the porch since I was a little girl was still there. I wasn't even fully inside the house yet, and I could smell the mothballs from the porch. That brought back familiar feelings as well because Sandra was known for having her home smelling like mothballs. The grass looked like it hadn't been cut in years because as we walked, the grass damn near came up to our ankles.

I remember as a little girl, there would be big ass frogs on the porch at night. So, as I walked and held onto my children's hands, I made sure that I flashed the light on my phone, just in case the three of us had to make a run for it. We were now standing on the porch, and I heard loud laughter coming from inside the house, making me believe that she had company. I guess that explained the extra two cars in the driveway. Some things never changed.

When I was a little girl, and my mom would be home on the weekends, since she claimed that the weekends were her off day from whatever she did during the week, she would always have her loud-mouthed friends over. They would be up until the wee hours of the morning, smoking, drinking, and playing cards or dominos. I hated when her friends came over because not only did I not get any sleep, but Summer and I would always have to clean up their mess in the morning. Because they would get so high off the drugs and so drunk from the liquor, it left the house in total disarray. I'm talking broken glass bottles all over the floor, and because their little card games would get so intense, sometimes I would wake up the next morning to seeing the wooden dining room table flipped over from someone growing so upset that they felt the need to flip the table.

At nine years old, I questioned myself about the powdery substance that I would always find on the table the next morning. It wasn't until I got older that I realized that coke was one of the drugs that Sandra had been engaging in all these years. It made me wonder if that drug was the reason why she would treat me the way she did. Thinking about all of that lowkey made me want to just turn around, but then I heard my kids yawn, so I knew that I had no choice but to knock on the door.

For five minutes straight, my kids and I banged on the door because it was so loud on the inside that they couldn't hear us banging.

"Okay, someone is coming now," I said after I saw a figure look out of the curtain that was next to the front door.

I couldn't really tell who the person was, but I knew that

it was a woman. I pulled my kids closer to me and released a nervous breath as I watched the doorknob turn. Once the door was open, I saw that it was Sandra's best friend, Anita, on the other side of the door. She lived a few houses down when I was a little girl, but I didn't know if she still stayed so close. Anita used to be a beautiful woman. Back then, Sandra couldn't do hair to save her life, so she would always call Anita over to do me and Summer's hair.

Anita always used to have pretty hairstyles, and I would always ask her to do my hair like hers, but the only thing that Sandra ever allowed me to wear was braids, so that's what I would get. Back then, Anita had all the name brand clothes like the people that I saw on music videos, her nails and feet were always done so nicely, her purse collection was out of this world, and she had a frame that I would beg God to allow me to have once I grew up. Now, she looked bad, and I wondered if it had anything to do with the drugs that I knew she had engaged in with Sandra.

She'd lost a lot of weight, making it look like her pants size had to have been a 00. The shirt that she wore was hung over her body, and even the tights she was wearing were too big for her. Her eyes were damn near sunken in to the point that I could see her bone structure. It killed me to see her like that because she was easily one of the most beautiful women that I'd ever met in my life at one time.

"Is this Winter? I know this isn't my little Winter. Oh my God, look at you! Look how beautiful you are," Anita said, as she reached out and she gave me a hug.

I hugged her back, but I didn't hug her as tight as she was hugging me because I was afraid that I would break her.

"Anita, who the hell is that at my door? I told you not to even open my motha fuckin' door in the first place because you know the only people who knock on the door on this side of town at this time of the night are fuckin' crack heads, and I don't have no money to be giving to no crackheads. Now, who—" Her voice stopped mid-sentence once she came to the door, stood right next to Anita, and realized that it was me at the door.

I swallowed a huge lump in my throat because I will admit that I was scared. Here I was, twenty-nine years old, just a few months away from seeing thirty, and standing there with my two children, yet I felt so powerless again. This woman had the power to make me feel like that helpless little girl that she had made me out to be for the majority of my childhood. I could even sense that my children were frightened because they had moved even closer to me. Funny thing is, neither of my children knew about Sandra or the horrible things that she'd done to me over the years. I wasn't sure if I would ever even tell them about my childhood because that was just one of those things that I didn't like to talk about.

Hell, a few months ago, Storm had walked into my bedroom while I was putting my shirt over my head, and she inquired about the leftover bruises that were on my back. I had to lie to my daughter and tell her that it was from falling years ago, but little did she know that those bruises came from years of getting the shit beat out of me like I was a slave.

"I know you done lost your mind bringing your ass to my doorstep! Let me guess, that nigga done kicked you out, right? When your ass left up of out here with him, I told you that's exactly what the fuck he was going to do, but your heard headed ass didn't listen. Your daddy did it, Anita's baby daddy did, so what made you think that you were exempt from a nigga leaving you high and dry? Let me guess, these are your kids from him, right? That's how they do it. Once you start pushing them kids out, gaining all that weight, and having all of them stretch marks take over your body, you become worthless to them.

"Look, I don't know what you came here for, but if you're asking me if you can move back in, the answer is no! I have two bedrooms here, one which belongs to me, and the other is for my wig collection. There's a women's homeless shelter about five blocks down which will be more than accommodating to you and your kids. Goodnight," she said while trying to slam the door in my face, but I put my foot out to stop her.

"Listen, I have nowhere else to go. Dewayne died in a car accident a week ago, and he left me with nothing. My name wasn't on anything; the house, the debit card, not even this car that I know is going to be taken any day now. I have nothing right now. Nothing to give my kids, and I can't even offer you anything if you allow us to come in here, but I promise I will get out and look for a job. I'm not asking for this to be a permanent stay, but I just need a few months to get back on my feet and save up enough money so to get an apartment.

"I've had my kids out since seven this morning, and they just need a place to lay their heads tonight. Even if you just let them stay, and I have to sleep outside in my car, that's fine with me. I just want them to get out of this car," I said with tears falling from my eyes as I released each word.

I was begging my own mother who'd brought me into this world to allow me and her grandchildren to come into her home.

"Ya'll can stay, but this isn't no fuckin' hotel, I hope you know that. This isn't a permanent stay either. I want the three of you out of my damn house in a matter of three months. I'm not giving up my wig room for ya'll, so you might as well make yourself comfortable on this damn couch. You want to move back in with me, well you know my rules, Winter. When you find a job, you will pay your dues around here. Oh, and the last thing, I'm not a god damn baby sitter either, so if you do find yourself a job, remember that I'm not watching shit! Hell, I didn't even want to watch you and your fuckin' sister, so what makes you think that I want to watch these two?" she fussed, and after she said all of those hurtful things, she finally walked away.

Anita gave me a look that screamed, "I'm sorry," and I just nodded because I already knew how this went. I had my kids stay on the porch while I went to the car and grabbed the two duffle bags from the back. Once I was walking back up the porch steps, I noticed that all the people in the house were leaving, including Anita. I recognized a few of the faces, and they gave me hugs, complimented my beautiful kids, and just like that, they'd left.

Now that I was in the house with my kids, I closed the front door. After that, I heard a door slam in the house, which I knew had to have come from Sandra's bedroom. I knew where the bathroom was, so that's where I walked to with the twins. Once inside, I took a seat on the toilet, placed my head in my hands, and I sighed.

"I don't want to stay here, Mommy. Can we go home?" my son cried as he walked over to me and wrapped his little arms around my neck.

"Me too, Mommy. Can we go home? I'm scared. I'm scared to be here. Let's go home, Mommyyy," my daughter cried.

I wrapped my arms around both of my babies and held them tight. Although at this moment I should have been their strength and should have been assuring them that everything was going to be okay, I just couldn't lie to my kids like that. I didn't know how this part of the story would end. I didn't know what job I would be able to find that would help pay the bills here, help me save up money for an apartment and pay for a baby sitter to watch the kids while I worked. I just didn't know.

One of the things I promised myself that I would never do was allow my kids to see a struggle, but in a matter of two weeks, I'd managed to break that promise.

CHAPTER EIGHT

"*Knock! Knock! Knock!*"

I was in the middle of looking at another property out in the Fort Lauderdale area when there was a loud knock on my office door. This particular property that I was looking at wasn't too far from the beaches, the malls, and the great restaurants in the Fort Lauderdale area. One would think that I had enough money and that I didn't have to purchase any more properties, but I was trying to have my hands in so many things that if I ever did have children later down the line, I could leave them with a legacy that would keep them financially stable.

Of course, I wanted kids; I just didn't want kids with any damn body. Kids were a reflection of their parents, so whatever woman I settled down with had to be someone who I would want my daughter to be like or someone who I would want my son to date when he was of age. When I found out that Amari was having my daughter, I swear I felt as if I'd just won the fuckin' lottery because I loved the thought of having a miniature version of my fiancée running around.

I knew that Amari would instill great values, morals, and confidence in my daughter, so I wasn't like most niggas who were afraid of having a little girl because I knew the type of parenting that my daughter would get. I say that because these days, niggas seem to fear the thought of having a daughter. It's not often that you hear a man talk about having a daughter, but I wasn't afraid of no shit like that. I knew Amari was going to be a great parent, and I knew that I would be the same.

Although I didn't have children of my own, I damn near raised Queen. When Queen was born, I was fourteen years old. I guess I forgot to mention that while my ole girl was pregnant with Queen, my ole boy was still knocking her around. Crazy thing is, neither Ocean nor I had known about my ole girl being pregnant until she was almost through with the pregnancy. To this day, I can't tell you if she was hiding the pregnancy or she didn't know just like we all didn't know because the pregnancy didn't stop my ole boy from hitting her, nor did it make her want to leave him so that she wouldn't miscarry.

A lot of shit went down in that fuckin' house that I still didn't have answers for, but even as an adult, I just didn't want to ask my ole girl certain shit. I had witnessed women coming in and out of the house during the wee hours of the morning, but my ole girl would be home while they were there. I saw a lot of shit, but just like I did everything else in my life that I wanted to run away from, I bottled all that shit up and pretended that it never even happened.

Anyways, like I was saying, as much as I wanted to have some little Boss juniors running around or a few princesses running around, I wasn't about to dump my seeds off in just anything. I was a different breed of nigga, so good, wet pussy couldn't have me making permanent life decisions. Once that fuck session was over, and all rocks were off, I would have to deal with that person for the rest of my life if I got the woman pregnant, and that just wasn't some shit that I was trying to have happen for me and my future.

These days, I had been thinking about the shit that my ole girl had told me a few weeks ago about settling down. Although I didn't give much of a response to her, that didn't mean I wasn't thinking about it. Back at my house, I had two dogs, which were a German Shepherd and an American Bully Pitbull. Both were females whose names were Bella and Marley. At my command, they would bite the fuck out of you. That's who I came home to at the end of a long work day. Those big ass dogs who came up to my thighs are who welcomed me home with open arms and looked forward to seeing me just as much as I looked forward to seeing them when I walked through the door.

Although that was an amazing feeling, I knew that coming home to an actual human being felt ten times better.

I knew that because I had that feeling before. Amari used to greet me at the door each time I came home from work. Food would be prepared, and pussy would be waiting on the counter for me to knock it out the frame. These new generational bitches were from a different breed, and I swear that shit wasn't a compliment.

All these bitches knew nowadays was UberEATS and fuckin' Postmates. It was almost like getting their asses in the kitchen to cook was a disease or some shit. I was a hood nigga, so I wasn't even expecting a woman to come home and cook me five-star meals every night because that was probably too perfect of a woman, and honestly, I wasn't looking for perfection. Spaghetti took twenty minutes, throw a cheap cube steak in the oven with some instant mash potatoes and instant corn, and that's a twenty-minute meal too. I swear a nigga wasn't asking for Martha Stewart around this bitch, but maybe just her long lost cousin for all I cared.

These females were too worried about shit like getting posted on social media and all that other bullshit that I felt wasn't important in a relationship. You see, Amari was old school because her mother was old school. Growing up, it was Amari, her ole girl, and her stepdad. She used to tell me how her ole girl would cook breakfast and dinner for her stepdad every morning and night. I remember her telling me how at times she would walk into their bedroom and see her mom massaging her step dad's feet, so when Amari and I were old enough, she started doing that same shit for me.

I did my part too, which was to make sure that everything she did for me, I would do double. Bitches get in relationships and think that it's just about their wants and their needs. As men, we wanted to be asked how our day was too. We could use a massage here and there, and we didn't have to always be the one to initiate sex. On some real shit, I could be in my man cave watching the game or something, and she could come in, pull my gym shorts and boxers down, and give a nigga some head or ride me to sleep.

The bitches I fucked just weren't mentally on the level that I was on, and they couldn't give me what I wanted, which was why I didn't take their asses serious. It wasn't even that I was looking for traits of Amari in another woman because, this time around, I wouldn't mind something different. But damn, I wasn't about to settle either.

Although people look at me as this cocky, mean ass nigga, I swear I wasn't asking for much. You didn't have to be a perfect woman for me to want to settle down with you. I wasn't looking for the woman with the littlest waist or the fattest ass for that matter because all of that was physical.

"Come in," I finally called out after pulling the camera footage up on my desktop and realizing that it was one of the assistant managers of this specific location of the housing apartments.

I was in the Miami office this morning, which was the first property I had bought. Out of all the properties, this one happened to be the one that I spent a lot of my time at. Shit was always happening at this property. Whether it was the tenants not paying their rent on time or violence happening late at night. This was a low-income area, so bad shit tended to happen, or just anything that would have made any other person give all this shit up a long time ago.

Trust me, the thought of selling this specific space had crossed my mind a thousand times, but I feared what the buyer would turn it into once I sold it. The buyer probably wouldn't have the same pure heart that I had or the same upbringing so they may not be able to sympathize with the single mothers living there and trying to do whatever she can to provide for her kids. My struggle was deeply rooted in me, which was the only reason why I hadn't sold this spot.

It was Kiondra on the other side of the door. Let's just say that Kiondra had good skills while she was on the job and good skills while she was off the job. I hired her about two years ago, and I didn't start fuckin' her until about six months after she started working for me. Kiondra was a beautiful woman with a good head on her shoulders, smart as hell, but shorty just wasn't the one for me. I didn't know if it was because of the whole business and pleasure thing not working out, but I tried to do the whole relationship thing with her, and I just couldn't.

Although shorty was classy as hell on the job, it seemed like all of that class went out the window once she clocked out. During our time together, I felt like she was insecure as a motha fucka. We could be out together, and I could literally look at a bitch for a second, and she would be jumping down my throat and asking me if I fucked the bitch. If I said no, then she would hit me with, "Well, you must want to fuck her then!"

I wasn't used to having women in my life clock me like that, amongst so much other shit, so I stopped fuckin' around with her like that. Her inability to be the girl I needed didn't have anything to do with her professional skills, so I kept her on the job. Of course, she still tried to fuck me every chance she got, but I wasn't doing that with her.

At one point, her feelings were involved, and I wasn't the type of nigga to play on women's feelings, so she wasn't getting any dick from me. She walked into my office holding papers in her hand and took a seat before me. I was a man, so when she sat down, and her breasts were damn near spilling out of the button up top that she was wearing, it was harder than a motha fucka for me not to look.

Kiondra was a chocolate woman with the prettiest white teeth that I'd ever seen. She had a nice hourglass shape, and she had the whole natural thing going on with her hair. Today, it was pulled back into a big, thick ass ponytail.

"We have a problem, Cortez," she said.

Everyone else around there referred to me as Mr. Anderson, but I guess since she knew what my dick tasted like, she felt that she could address me by my first name, even though I'd checked her on that so many times before.

"Mr. Anderson, but go ahead and continue," I jumped in, cutting her off.

She gave me a look that screamed how badly she wanted to roll her eyes at me, but she didn't roll them, which was good on her part. She released a sigh and then put the paperwork in front of me, which was printed out Excel documents of the tenants' rent payments for the last three months.

"This is March, February, and January's rent statements. As you can see, the tenant in apartment 3606 hasn't been paying her rent for the last few months. I know you're probably going to get mad, especially since I didn't bring this info to you the first month when I noticed that she didn't pay, but I didn't know what you would say. I guess I feared you not having sympathy with her and putting her out. She just had a newborn baby a month ago along with the other three children that she already has, so I told her that she could wait to come up with the money for the rent and—"

"Get me the keys for that unit," I said, standing up from the chair that I was sitting in and picking up my suit jacket as well.

I buttoned up my suit and followed Kiondra out the door as she went down the hall, which was where we kept all the spare keys for the units. It didn't take but a few seconds for the keys to be in my hands and for me to let her know that I would be back. This is the shit that I was talking about when I said that this specific property always had some shit going on. I was the owner, yet here I was about to make a social call.

I walked over to the apartment building and took the stairs up to the third floor. As soon as I reached the front of the door, I heard kids on the inside crying and a mother screaming for them to be quiet. I just took the key with me as a backup, but I had no plans to walk inside this woman's personal space. I felt like I was banging on that fuckin' door for five minutes before it finally opened.

There stood a mother, looking directly at me, and seeing her face gave me flashbacks of my mother from when I was a little boy. It was the middle of the day, and she was still in her pajamas. She was sporting a black eye along with a busted lip, and because she was wearing a tank top, I could see the many scratches that were on her neck and chest area, making it look like she'd gotten into a fight with a cat. She was holding onto a small baby, and with the door opened, I could see two other children in the back who were playing with toys, oblivious to the fact that I was even standing at the front door.

"Please don't kick me out. I promised Kiondra that I would have the money for all three months by next week. I'm just waiting to get my refund. I didn't think that it would take this long," she said, and I could hear the hurt, pain, and desperation in her voice.

"Who the fuck is that at the damn door? Bitch, didn't I tell your silly ass to keep the fuckin' door closed? Who the fuck—"

His voice cut off when he saw me. My eyes went from his eyes to the wheelchair that he was in, only to see that he now had one leg. A part of me wanted to jump up and down and laugh at his karma, but another part of me didn't because all I had to do was stand there before him in this two thousand dollar Armani suit and let my presence speak for itself.

I hadn't seen him since the night he was arrested, and the night my ole girl checked us into the shelter. Truth be told, I thought his ass was dead because after all these years, I never ran into him again, so it was almost like he'd disappeared off the face of the Earth. He looked bad. Physically, he was nowhere near the same person that he was years ago. It had nothing to do with him having just one leg either because if anything, he looked sickly. He was no longer that big, cocky nigga who used to sit his ass in front of the TV with a belt draped around his neck, ready to use it on one of us. His head was now completely bald, he was very thin, and there were a lot of deep sores in his face, probably scaring the shit out of these kids.

"Fuck is this little nigga doing here? Fuck is you in front of my door for, boy?" he asked while wheeling himself closer to me.

Once he was close enough, he reached out and pushed the woman from in front of the door, and there we were, staring each other down. The last time we stared each other down like this, I ended up jumping in to fight him after he'd broken Ocean's arm. As a result of that, I ended up getting my ass fucked up with a broken jaw to match. This time, I could bet you my last dollar that not a motha fuckin' thing would break on me this time.

"Do I look like a little nigga to you? Fuck you mean your front door? Fuck nigga, this is MY front door! I own this shit! If this your shit, cough up three months of rent for me right now because your shit is three months behind," I said, and he didn't have shit to say. All he could do was raise his hand and wave me off like what I was saying was bullshit.

"I'm a little bit upset because I was really hoping that your ass was dead and somewhere rotting in hell. I see not much has changed with you either. You still going around putting your hands on women, huh? I hope that woman in there finds the strength to kick your ass out of this wheelchair and beat the fuck out of you with it!" I voiced with so much hate dripping from my voice as I spoke to him.

"The same way I had your mama wrapped around my finger is the way that I have that little bitch in there, so trust me, she's not going to do shit! You think you big shit now, huh? You put a little suit on, get a little muscle, and you think you can talk to me any kind of way. Little nigga, I'm still your motha fuckin' daddy! I'll still make you take off your clothes and put your hands on the wall, and beat your ass. Strip, nigga!" he yelled, followed by a laugh. "Remember that, huh?" he asked.

"You not even worth a reply. Look at you! You are in true form the pussy that you have always been. I just want you to know that me, your other two kids, and that beautiful woman that you used to beat on every day are shitting on your entire life right now! A part of me wants to come up out of this suit right now and beat your ass, but how the fuck would I look beating your ass and you don't even have two legs? Tell your lady that her rent for the rest of the month is on me. Make sure you let shorty know that I got her because it's obvious that you don't," I sarcastically let him know right before I walked away from the front door.

I knew that it hurt his pride like a motha fucka to know that his own son, someone who he probably hated just as much as I hated him, had to be the one to help keep the roof over his head. I could have been an asshole and kicked them all out, but why the fuck would I do that to them kids? Knowing that this man was alive and not that far from me was a feeling that I didn't like. I didn't like knowing that this nigga was laid up in one of the apartment buildings that I owned. As much as I didn't like it, I had to tell myself that he was going to continue getting his karma, so I would just stay back and let the shit unfold the way that it was going to.

CHAPTER NINE

THREE MONTHS LATER

"Come on, baby. Let Mommy put your shoes on," I whispered to my daughter as I kneeled before her and struggled to put on her house shoes.

It was one in the morning, and I'd just gotten off the bus and took the ten-minute walk to Anita's house after a long work day/night. Sandra was dead serious when she said that she wasn't going to babysit my children. Luckily, Anita stepped in and offered to watch them while I worked. She didn't even ask for anything in return, but I would still give her a little something here and there, which really wasn't much because I honestly didn't have much to give.

I was back working at Walmart as a stock clerk. Luckily, the manager was still working there from when I'd quit years ago. Because she had a little sympathy for me once I told her that I now had two children that I needed to provide for, she ended up hiring me on the spot, and I was back working like I'd never even left.

I worked every single day except Sunday. My work shift started at 4:00 p.m., and I would get off most nights by midnight. It really just depended on the amount of work that we had. I didn't too much care for the hours because it took away time that I was supposed to spend with my children, but at least I was able to earn money and provide for them the best way that I knew how.

Literally one week after I moved in with Sandra, I happened to have been looking out of the window, and I saw a tow truck come and haul my car away. There was literally no more fight left in me, so when I saw them doing that, all I could do was watch as cold tears dripped from my face because, yet again, I was failing my children. Although I was pretty much prepared for the car to be taken from me, especially since it wasn't in my name, I just didn't think that it would have happened so soon.

Honestly, that was minor compared to the hell on Earth that I was living in with Sandra. It's like she was making me earn the spot that my kids and I had in her home. It had been three months, and she still had us sleeping on the couch in her living room. She treated us like we were diseases. We couldn't eat any of her food or use any of her silverware, so I was actually surprised that she even let us use the guest bathroom to take baths and stuff.

Anything that the children ate, I had to purchase it. She had me paying the rent along with the electric bill. Although I was putting money to the side, I still felt like it wasn't enough for me to get out of there any time soon. It wasn't even an option to move in with Anita because she lived in a two bedroom apartment with her thirty-six-year-old son, so even if I moved in with her, I would be on the couch, so I might as well stay where I was. Plus, Anita already did so much for me, so I didn't want to be a burden and move in with her too. I wanted to at least have some type of dignity left.

"Mommy, I'm sleepy. I'm sleepy, Mommyyy," Storm whined after I had her shoes on.

With the kids' backpack on my back with all of their things in it for the night, I lifted Storm from the couch and grabbed my son's hand, who was standing behind me and being a big boy. I loved my kids to death, but my daughter always gave me the hardest time compared to her brother. Although they were only three, it was like it had registered in my son's head that Mommy was struggling with them, so he rarely complained. Even right now, I could see the tiredness all in his eyes, but he didn't utter a word.

Anita didn't have a car, nor did her son, so once we were out the door, it was time for us to walk back to the bus stop. I wanted to jump up and down with glee the moment we got to the bus stop, and the bus started coming. I used the bus card that I now had, and in no time, I was walking to the back with my kids. We found a spot, and Storm sat on my lap with her arms wrapped around my neck as she slept. Dewayne Jr sat next to me, crashing his head on my shoulder. A mother who felt like I had the weight of the world on my shoulders, I ended up throwing my head on the back of the seat and fighting with myself to stay up because I was so damn tired.

By the grace of God, I woke up in time to pull the string for my stop. Luckily, the drop off was in the area where Sandra's house was, so once we got off, we were literally in the house within ten minutes. Any other time when I got inside the house, I would lay the kids down on the couch while I went to shower, but it was something about today that had me tired as shit.

I had worked from the moment I clocked in, with only a thirty-minute break until the moment that I had clocked out. My feet were killing me in the off-brand Converse sneakers that I'd purchased from Payless a couple months ago. Because of my exhaustion, I dropped down on the couch with my babies once we were inside the house, never even taking off my shoes.

ONE HOUR LATER

"Winter, wake the hell up, girl! Get up, Winter!" I heard Sandra's loud ass voice as she stood over me, sounding like she was screaming at the top of her lungs for me to wake up.

It was a struggle, but my eyes finally opened, and they fought to stay open due to the light that she now had on in the living room mixed with the fact that I was still very much tired. I looked at the clock on the wall and saw that it was a little bit after 3:00 A.M. I was lying on the couch, still in my shoes, with one of my kids on either side of me.

They were both knocked out as I lay there with eyes on Sandra, demanding to know what the hell she wanted. She stood before me in one of her house gowns and a pink bonnet on her head. Crazy thing is, she looked exactly like how she did four years ago when I left. I couldn't say that she'd put on any weight, neither did she lose any. She still had that perfect, hourglass frame that she used to flaunt around. She still wore long weaves that went past the middle of her back, and although it was the year 2018, she still had that one gold tooth in her mouth like we were still in the '80s, which was when she'd gotten it.

I'll be the first to say that I had a beautiful mother, but it was her soul that made her look so ugly.

"What happened, Sandra?" I asked, wiping the sleepiness away from my eyes.

I watched my tone when it came to her because if my voice was over its normal octave, she would swear up and down that I had an attitude, and that would be her way to pick a fight with me. As badly as I wanted to go off on her for waking me up out of my much-needed sleep, I didn't.

"What happened is that your bad ass kids have been in my room again taking candy off my dresser, even after I told them to stay their little asses out of there. That's not even the cause of my anger right now, though. My problem is that you let those kids do what the fuck they want to do without addressing it or disciplining them! Do you see that fuckin' bathroom? They have their little toys all over the fuckin' floor in there, their towels are on the floor and everything. You need to get your ass up and go clean that bathroom," she demanded.

I knew for a fact that she was being dramatic because the toys that my kids used to play with while they took their baths were back inside the tub. Plus, I'd folded their towels and put them on the rack before we left this afternoon for me to go to work, so I knew that she was just picking a fight with me. This was something that she often did so she could have victory in knowing that she kicked us out. I was smart, so I wasn't going to fall for her little ass tricks.

"Okay, I'll clean it in the morning. I'll even replace the candy that they took," I let her know.

"No, you'll do the shit right fuckin' now! I'm sick of this shit, Winter. I went from having this place to myself, to all of a sudden having three extra guests that I didn't want or need here with me. I'm sick of you and these retarded ass kids—"

"Whoa! Say whatever the hell you want to say to me, but please leave my children out of this—"

"Or what? What the fuck are you going to do if I don't leave them out of this? You brought them into this shit when you knocked on my fuckin' door begging me for a place to stay. As long as you're in my house, soaking up all of my good air, I can say whatever the fuck I want to say about you and these fuckin' kids!" she yelled back at me.

I was surprised that my children didn't wake up due to all the yelling that she was doing. Any other time, I would have just ignored her, but these were my babies that we were talking about, so I couldn't just pretend that what she just said never happened.

"Why do you have to be so hateful? You never loved me, so I understand that, but what did my kids do to you? Hearing you call them retarded is similar to the things that you used to say to me, but much worse. What caused you to be like this?" I just had to ask her because I really wanted to know.

Yes, my children should have never taken the candy out of her room because she was right, she had been telling them to stop doing that, and I have been telling them the same thing. But it didn't give her the right to disrespect them. She acted as if she hated them, and honestly, she didn't even know them that well to hate them. She didn't even know my kids' names. If she needed them to do something for her, she would just state what she needed, never calling them by their names, which was how I knew that she didn't remember their names from when I'd told them to her.

"I don't owe you no fuckin' explanation, Winter. You can either clean my fuckin' bathroom, or you can get the hell out; you choose. Coming in here questioning me! You need to be thanking me for giving your stupid ass a place to stay. Over here launching these kids off from house to house in the wee hours of the fuckin' morning. What type of fuckin' mother do you call yourself! I don't feel bad for you one bit because you did this to these fuckin' children. You let that man come into your life, whisper to you a bunch of sweet nothing lies, and in the end, you got left with two fuckin' kids that you can't even take care of! If that's not stupid, then I don't know what it is! You have some fuckin' nerve telling me to watch my mouth about your kids when you didn't even watch the life that you were living. If you had, you wouldn't be sleeping on this fuckin' couch right now!" she voiced.

"Shut up! You don't know a damn thing! Excuse me if I fell for the first person who ever told me that they loved me! Besides Dewayne, I never had anyone tell me that they loved me. Never!" I yelled, and my voice cracked. Although I tried not to, I began to cry. "I loved the feeling of someone telling me that they loved me, so yes, I fell for it. You question what type of mother I am, and the answer to that is a mother who is willing to do whatever the hell I have to do for my children, even if that means being degraded, talked down upon, and made to feel worthless by the very same woman who brought me into this world. That's called mothering, something your ass doesn't know shit about!

"As you can see, I'm already down, so why knock me down some more? I'm a better mother than you will ever be, and a part of me feels like you know that, which is why you're so jealous of me" I said, and she burst out laughing in my face.

Her outburst caused the kids to wake up. I could tell

from the looks on their faces that they were scared. My kids literally feared this woman. Their little eyes bucked, and they scooted closer together and wrapped their arms around each other as they watched what was about to unfold in front of them.

"Jealous of what? I'm twice your age, and I still look better than you, sweetheart. I wish the fuck I would be jealous of you with that cow looking ass skin you have. The way that man of yours just treated you, I can't relate because any guy that I've ever messed around with has worshipped the ground that my pretty feet have walked on. If you weren't so damn stupid and naïve, I would have taught you the game and showed you that you don't love these niggas because they don't love us. When you love these dog ass niggas out here, you end up just another baby mama, and you walk around here looking like a sad puppy. Look at you. Hair all over your head, nails not done, I can only imagine what your toes look like. I learned years ago from your bitch ass daddy that men weren't shit. I should have gone ahead with the abortion when I was given the chance," she hatefully said, sounding like her old self.

I can't tell you the many times she's thrown in my face that when she found out she was pregnant with me, my dad had told her to get an abortion, but she'd refused to. Any chance she got, she let it be known that she should have taken his advice. The fact that she went through with the pregnancy and actually brought me into this world had a lot to do with the way she treated me. She basically resented me.

"Come on, ya'll. Junior, help your sister put on her shoes," I said as I stood up from the couch and folded the blanket that the three of us shared.

Their backpack that was on the carpet, along with the two duffle bags, I grabbed them up, moving as quickly as possible for the three of us to get out of there. I just couldn't take it anymore. For months, I'd been taking the disrespect because I was doing this for my children, but this was it.

The whole time I moved around getting our things together and helping the kids with their things, she stood there laughing and talking all the shit in the world that she could talk.

"You prove to me every day just how dumb you are. It's three in the damn morning so I would like to know just where in the hell are you taking these damn kids? You have no fuckin' money, no place to stay, so where are you going? Let me guess, Anita's house? If you go over there with these little kids, where she has that grown ass man sleeping in the back room, then you really are dumb. Your ass is weak, Winter, just like your damn father. What, you going to run away because I said a few things that you didn't want to hear?" she asked me.

With everything in my hands, I stood in front of her. I was so close to her that I could feel the heat from her breath when she breathed.

"I'm not leaving because I'm weak. I'm actually leaving because I'm stronger than this. After twenty-nine years, it's about time that I know my worth. I came to you with my children, and the only thing that I had was the clothes on my back along with a few other outfits in this bag. I drove around for hours, contemplating if I wanted to come here or not because I knew the hateful person that you are. Even as hateful as you are, I was hoping that you could find it in your heart to give us a place to stay, just until I got my shit together.

"Like my kids and me don't have the same blood as you running through our body, you've treated us like shit from the moment you let us into your home. In your guest bedroom, where your wig collection is, you have a whole king sized bed in there that you could have easily allowed us to sleep in, but no, you chose to let us sleep on a couch that feels like we're sleeping on bricks. I guess I shouldn't complain because at least you gave us a place to stay, huh?

"I actually don't know where the hell I'm going. I'll sleep up under a damn bridge with my children before I come back and sleep in this house with you. I apologize for my kids and I being a burden to you. Most importantly, I apologize for being the daughter that you wish you didn't have. I'm sorry for ruining your life, and from this day forward, I promise you won't have to worry about seeing my children or me again. Goodbye, Sandra," I finished while I walked around her, and my kids followed.

There was nothing else that needed to be said. Truth be told, I should have never come over there in the first place, but I guess you can say that this was a lesson learned. I thought about going to Anita's place, but as soon as the thought came into my mind, it went out because I couldn't stand to be around her son, Gary. He was weird as hell, and every time I came over to either drop the kids off or pick them up, he was always staring at me with those creepy eyes. I've heard Sandra say a few times to her friends that he was mentally challenged, but I honestly didn't know if that was true or not.

"Where are we going, Ma?" Junior asked me after we took the five-minute walk to the bus stop.

"I'm not sure, baby. I'm honestly not sure," I let him know, and he sadly nodded.

Almost ten minutes had gone by before the bus finally came. When the three of us got on, it was only three other people on the bus who looked as if they'd just gotten off from work. Like always, we took our seat in the back, and the moment my ass hit the seat, I placed my head on the window and quietly looked out. My head was turned away from my children because I didn't want them to see that I was crying. I was crying because a place for us to stay tonight had finally popped in my head, but the fact that I would even have to do this with my kids was what had me so emotional. They just didn't deserve it.

After almost fifteen minutes on the bus, I finally pulled the cord so we could get off at our spot. Walking fast as hell because this just wasn't the best area for us to be in at this time of the night, we finally made our way inside. We were at my job. A place that I knew was open 24 hours. It was four in the morning, so no one was really in the store like that. I knew that the general managers were more than likely off right now, so I didn't have to worry about them catching me.

With my kids, I casually, walked inside the store, and I headed for the staircase so we could go in the break room. The breakroom was empty, and I noticed that it had been cleaned for the night. I closed and locked the door behind me, making it where no one would be able to get inside unless I opened the door for them.

"We're going to sleep here, Mommy?" Storm asked with excitement dripping from her little voice.

Crazy how my baby would much rather sleep here than to sleep at her own grandmother's house. I took a seat on the cold, tiled floor, pulled both of them down with me, and wrapped my arms around them.

"Just for tonight. Mommy will figure it out in the morning. I promise," I let both of them know.

"You don't have to promise us anything, Mommy," Junior spoke up and said.

I nodded at his words, and then I leaned over and kissed them both on their little cheeks.

There's a woman's homeless shelter about five blocks down, which will be more than accommodating to you and your kids. Sandra's words surfaced again in my head from the night that I'd come over to her house with my kids asking her for a place to stay.

I knew the shelter that she was referring to because I passed it every afternoon on my way to drop the kids off at Anita's house. I guess going there tonight hadn't crossed my mind until just now. First thing tomorrow morning, I was going to head down there with my kids to see if they had enough room for the three of us. There was no way in hell I would get these kids up again and put them on a bus, so I'd just wait to do it tomorrow and just go there with high hopes that they would be able to accommodate us. If there wasn't enough room, I really didn't know what I was going to do, and because I didn't know, that reason alone caused me to not get any sleep.

Both of my kids were laid out with their little heads in my lap while I sat up and had a long conversation with God. The whole time I prayed, I placed my hands on my kids' heads and asked God to keep the three of us safe in His graces and for better days to be on the way for us.

CHAPTER TEN

"Neeoooo, I'm about to cummmm... Shittt, I'm cumminnnggg... I'mm cumminggg!" I screamed, damn near cried at the top of my lungs as my husband stood behind me and penetrated me from the back.

I didn't know how to feel about him coming home and fucking me like this. My husband had been gone for the last three days on a business trip, and once he walked through the door, which was a little bit after seven this morning, I had been bouncing around on his dick ever since. Don't get me wrong, sex with my husband wasn't something that didn't take place almost every day, but it was something about the way he had my legs pinned behind my head this morning. Something about the way he was digging in my guts this morning that had me crying. I was built Ford tough, so I never cried while taking the dick.

He held me so tight, paid attention to every single part of my body, and he was more talkative during our sex this morning, telling me how much he loved me, which was a little different from the sexcapades that we would have any other day. Don't get me wrong, I liked it, but I just wanted to know why. I felt like he was fuckin' me this way because he was guilty about something, so the moment I came down from this orgasmic high, I started with my bullshit, as he likes to call it whenever I questioned him about something.

"I should have smelled your dick before you started fuckin' me," I said, throwing the covers off me and sitting up in the bed.

I couldn't find the pajamas that I had on right before he'd stripped me of all my clothes, so I reached over and retrieved his tank top that he had on under his shirt not too long ago.

"There you go with that bullshit, Ocean. Smell my dick for what? Only thing you were going to smell on it was the Dove soap that I used this morning to wash it off before I got on the damn plane. You always bitching about something. I haven't been in this bitch for one whole hour, and you already trying to start something up with a nigga. I guess I can forget about asking you to cook me some breakfast, huh?" he asked as he stepped into his Versace boxers that he'd just come out of. My juices were still on his dick, as he put it away.

I looked up at my husband, and I'll admit that my heart

skipped a few beats like it always did when I watched him. Neo was the finest man walking this green Earth to me. I saw my mother in law a few days ago, and I made sure that I thanked her for the thousandth time for bringing something so perfect into this world. My man had a high yellow skin tone, that would easily get marked up when I was on top of him, riding him into the sunset, as I clawed my long nails that I loved to wear deep into his neck, back, or anything that I could find. I was a kisser, so it wasn't out of the ordinary to see him with his body riddled with the marks of passion that I loved to keep on him.

Along with that beautiful skin, he had long ass dreads that he'd been growing ever since he was fifteen. My brother and Neo took going to the gym very serious, so just like Boss, Neo looked as if he could sell DVDs on how to get that perfect, muscular body that he had along with those washboard abs. Although my husband was a businessman, that didn't deter the many tattoos that he had on his body. My favorite one just happened to be the portrait of myself that was located on the right side of his upper chest area.

One would look at my husband, and people just assumed that he was hood or ghetto because of his appearance, but what they didn't know was that he was actually a hood and ghetto millionaire. Neo and I loved hookah, so it was no surprise when he opened his first lounge almost four years ago. What started off as just one lounge, which happened to be the best lounge in Miami, turned into him opening three more. Now, he was trying to expand into other cities like Las Vegas, Los Angeles, and next month, he had a trip planned to Colorado, where he wanted to look at potential buildings there as well.

My husband was a great man, a wonderful provider, but I'll be damned if I didn't have my insecurities when it came to him.

I'd been with Neo ever since I was seventeen years old. When I lost my virginity to him at eighteen, he was the cause of my dad slamming me and breaking my arm when he saw the hickies that were left on my neck, which I thought I'd did a good job of hiding, but I guess not. Talking about my dad and the shit that he used to do to us when we were younger takes me to a dark place so I won't elaborate much on that. Just know that I'm thankful for myself, my brother, and my mom to even be alive because the three of us sure did endure our fair share of beatings.

Anyway, over the years that I've been with my husband, he hasn't always been faithful towards me. All the infidelities mostly happened in our twenties when we weren't married yet. I've caught this man texting other bitches, entertaining other bitches, or even telling me he was going one place, but would actually be at another place. I caught him doing everything but actually fuckin' the bitch, which was good on everybody's part because there is no doubt in my mind that I would be in jail for murder if I ever saw some shit like that with my own two eyes.

Damn right there were times when I wanted to get some get back and fuck on another nigga just like he had been doing. But when I told him during sex that this was his pussy, I actually meant that, so I couldn't go astray even if I wanted to. Plus, I didn't have it in me to cheat. I couldn't just have sex with a person and let it be just sex. With sex, feelings were involved, and it was a form of connecting with someone, so I just couldn't do it the way men were able to have sex and let it just be that.

Back when my husband used to cheat, he would always say that he didn't have feelings for the bitches that he would fuck around on me with. It was so fuckin' weird to me how a man could do that. That's the past, though, and I didn't think that my husband was cheating on me these days. I knew bitches still tried to shoot their shot with him because half the time, he would tell me, but from what my husband tells me, he doesn't pay them any attention.

The way we just fucked this morning brought back too many memories of the past. Back then, when we were just boyfriend and girlfriend, he would do things to my body that would have me limping the next morning, and it wouldn't be long before text messages would be sent to my phone from a bitch telling me how she was with my man not too long ago. Whenever Neo would come home and do my body like this, it would usually end in some bullshit. That's why this morning, I was sitting right there questioning his motives.

"You know why I would want to smell your dick, Neo. Stop acting fuckin' crazy! Any other time your ass comes in the house this time of the morning, you go straight to sleep. Why did you fuck me like that this morning, then?" I asked, jumping up from the bed and getting in his face.

He ran his hand down his face and pulled on his beard,

that looked as if it was getting longer and fuller by the damn day.

"I swear your ass is fuckin' crazy. Wasn't you just sending me all those freaky ass text messages, pictures, and videos these past few days, telling me how you miss a nigga and how you couldn't wait until I came back home because you were horny? I tried to book you a flight last night to come and see me, but you were screaming that I'm tired bullshit. I swear to God we need to get your ass checked out because you are so fuckin' bipolar, man. Fuck!" he yelled and punched his hand down on the bed.

I knew my husband. I'm talking the type of knowing that Lebron James knew for the game of basketball, so I knew that something was going on and I that the truth was going to come out. Any other time, he would wave off what I was saying, and he wouldn't get so uptight about my accusations, but the fact that he was turning blood red and was getting so defensive proved to me that something happened.

I walked over to him and quickly straddled his lap. I pulled his undershirt that I was wearing up and over my ass then grabbed his hands, placing them directly on my ass. He squeezed my cheeks together and looked at me with tired eyes although I could feel his dick poking through the fabric of his boxers, dying to be freed. My hands went around his neck, and I stared deep into his eyes.

"If you have something to tell me, Neo, you better tell me now because you know that I always find out. I'm not that same, gullible twenty-year-old that you could do anything to. I'm a grown ass woman, so if you cheated on me while you were away, I swear to God that you will lose your wife. I swear," I said, looking him in his eyes because I needed him to know how serious I was right now.

"Baby, I swear I didn't do shit. Fuck would I do some shit like that to you, especially when you know what we just went through last month?" he said, making me lose the cold glare that I had on him.

I had a miscarriage last month. A very bad miscarriage. Sometimes when I walked into this bedroom, I swear I could still smell the blood that was pouring out of me when it was happening. I'd literally just made it to the second semester the day of the miscarriage, and I was planning to tell my sister, my brother, and my mom, but in moments, I'd lost my baby. I wasn't fully back to the person that I was before it, but I was getting there.

I thought about what Neo had just said to me, and I guess I believed him. I would hope that he wouldn't do me dirty, especially at a time like this. I didn't bother responding to him, though. Instead, I just raised myself from his lap and proceeded to the bathroom that was in our bedroom to take a shower and get ready for today. The moment I made it inside the bathroom, I looked in the mirror, taking my appearance all the way in.

I was tall with a slim frame, standing 5'9". All my life, I was told that I should get into modeling, but I wished like hell I would've asked my mom to put me into modeling when I was younger, especially with the way that we were struggling back then. I had a natural, sandy brown hair color, which stopped just a few inches before the middle of my back. I usually wore my hair in wraps or braids from time to time. Like my brother, I had beautiful, light brown eyes, a few tattoos here and there, most of which were small. Often, I was compared to the R&B singer Keri Hilson, just smaller and without the hazel eyes.

I knew I was beautiful, but I think as women, we all go through that phase of just not feeling good enough or that phase of insecurities and depression. I don't care what anyone says, losing a baby is something that can bring the hardest woman down to her knees. I was strong because of the way that my childhood was growing up. I had withstood far too many physical ass whoopings for me to be weak, so these days, there wasn't much shit that would faze me, but to actually feel every pain that I felt when my baby died was something, man. Something that I was still battling with.

Even right now, look at me, as I was hiding in the bathroom from my husband so he wouldn't see that I was still crying over this, and it had been a month already. To make matters worse, I was around children damn near all the time with me being partners with my mom at the shelter. I saw everything from newborn babies to teenagers, and that didn't do anything but increase my desire to have children of my own. I was aware of the fact that my day would soon come, but shit, I was scared to try again.

After taking a very hot shower and doing everything else that I needed to do to get ready for work, I was about to walk out of the bedroom, but I stopped and looked at my husband one last time. He knew that I was getting ready to head out to work, so he was sleeping on my side of the bed because in his words, he liked to smell my scent whenever I wasn't physically sleeping right next to him.

Any other time, I would have walked over, kissed him, and let him know that I was leaving, but I didn't do either of the two. In a matter of seconds, I just turned on my heels and walked out the door. Once I was outside, I jumped in my 2018 red, Lexus IS 250 that my husband purchased for me last year as a birthday gift. Like always, I drove with the Pandora radio station on Monica as I made my way to the shelter.

It was Saturday morning, so I already knew that today was going to be a long day. Weekends were always the busiest day of the week, which was the only reason why I was heading in so early. Because I knew how today would go, I made sure to stop at Starbucks to get me and my mom our favorite Frappuccino along with two muffins.

When I finally pulled up to the shelter and saw the line, I released a sigh because here we were again. Like every weekend, the line was wrapped around the building. When I got out of the car, I made sure that I spoke to everyone as I made my way inside. Like always, I just walked into my mom's office like all of her children did when we came in. She looked up from the paperwork that she was studying, and with her glasses resting on her face, she watched me as I walked closer to her desk.

"I would ask if Neo made it back safely into town, but judging by your walk, you pretty much answered my question," she called out, referring to the limp that I came in with.

We couldn't put shit past our mama because her ass just managed to know everything. She knew when I lost my virginity. After the miscarriage, she'd told me that she knew that I was pregnant all along but just didn't say anything since she knew that I was trying to surprise them. It wasn't much that we could surprise her with because she was always on top of everything, especially when it came to her kids.

I gave a phony laugh to her statement as I sat before her and passed her the Frappuccino and the bag because I'd already eaten my muffin on the way over. I drank from the straw as all type of shit went through my head.

"What's wrong with you, Ocean?" my mom finally asked me.

There was a long pause because I wanted to think about my words before I just started spitting things out. I didn't too much care to come to my mom about marital problems with Neo and I because I felt like I've already overwhelmed her with so much over the years regarding my relationship with him. I was in my twenties, wrapped up in her arms and crying to her about getting cheated on yet again by Neo. I damn sure wouldn't go to my brother with the problems that I had with Neo because they were best friends, and I didn't want to put a damper on their friendship.

When Neo and I got together, that was one of the things that Boss was worried about. Boss was so overprotective when it came to the ones he loved, so he felt like I was putting him in a fucked-up position by getting with his best friend because, at the end of the day, his loyalty would always lie with me since I was blood. He just didn't want to beef with Neo if things were to one day get out of line between us.

Boss knew about the cheating that Neo would do on me because I would tell him. His response was always, "If you not planning on leaving the nigga, then don't come to me with that." I never left, so after a while, Boss told me to stop getting him involved in our shit. The first time Neo cheated on me, I told my brother on him, and I remember them in the living room of my mama's apartment fighting, breaking lamps, even making the 75-inch TV fall over that was mounted on the TV stand. They did all of that, only for me to get right back with him the next week. After that, Boss pretty much just stayed out of it, which was understandable.

Don't laugh at me ladies, because we all have had that one man in our life who had us saying that we swear that we were done with them, only for us to come running back days later. I shook those thoughts from my head and focused on the matter at hand. I figured that there really wasn't a right way to say how I was feeling, so I just spit it right on out.

"I think Neo is cheating on me," I blurted out, and she sighed along with rolling her eyes.

"Ocean, please! Did you figure that out before or after you let him have sex with you this morning? Neo isn't crazy enough to cheat on you again, especially after I put that threat in his ear the last time that he went astray," she went on to say.

I didn't know what my mom had said to Neo years ago,

but all I knew was that once she had talked to him, the cheating had stopped. I literally never had any more problems with him after that.

"Ma, sex this morning was just so different. I could feel that he was guilty about something, but I just don't know what it is. When he walked in the room this morning, I could see it all in his face that something was wrong. I know my husband, Ma. Therefore, I know that he's keeping something from me. As badly as I want this marriage to work, and as badly as I want to have children, Ma, I'm telling you if he fucked around on me while he was away, I'm walking. I'm not going to fight him on it, I'm not going to question him why I'm just going to simply have the lawyers draw up some divorce papers, and I'm out. I'm thirty-five years old, Ma. You know how crazy I would look if I were still out here getting cheated on?" I asked, my voice going up a few octaves because I was getting angry at just the thought of this shit.

"Only way for you to find out, Ocean, is for you to simply ask. But, for some reason, I can just feel it in my heart that you are overexaggerating. That man has way too much to lose for him to be going out to different cities and messing around with another woman," she assured me.

I thought about what she said, and I just nodded, leaving the conversation alone. At least, for now, I was going to. For another five minutes or so, I stayed back in the office until one of the workers came in and said that they were short staffed up front with the check-in services, so I announced that I would help. It was now four other women and me up front checking in the different women who were coming in the shelter with hopes of finding a place to stay.

We had plenty of space so they wouldn't have to worry about getting turned around. My phone buzzed in my back pocket, and I looked at it quickly, only to see that it was Neo. He was texting me to let me know that he loved me, and he would be down here later to bring me lunch. I didn't even bother to respond.

When I put the phone up, the baby fever that I had went through the roof as my eyes landed on a pair of twins, which were a little boy and a little girl. I instantly started smiling because they both were both so adorable. The little girl had a head full of hair that was in two huge ponytails. Although her hair needed to be combed, I swear she was still so damn perfect. Even the little boy had a head full of hair. His was in some fuzzy braids that were going to the back, and my ovaries screamed as I looked at the two of them.

My eyes fell from them and landed on who had to have been their mother because they looked exactly like her. One look at her and, I could tell that she was exhausted. She had beautiful, hazel eyes, but they were red, probably from lack of sleep, and just like a lot of the mothers that came in, I could tell from the look on her face that she was embarrassed about having to come here with her children.

I remembered when we had to come to a shelter when I was eighteen years old. I remembered looking around and praying to God that I didn't see anyone in there who would know me. All the other women up front with me were already occupied with other families, and because I was the only one free, the three of them made their way over to me.

"Hello. Welcome to Women and Kids shelter. Will it just be the three of you staying here?" I asked, putting on my professional voice.

One would have never known that something was going on with me or that I had a lot on my mind for that matter.

"Yes, it's just going to be us three," the woman said as she set the bags down next to her that she was originally holding in her hands.

"Okay. I'll just need your name along with the kids' names," I said while pulling out one of the forms that I would need for proper documentation of all the residents.

"My name is Winter Rivera, and my kids' names are Storm Stewart and Dewayne Stewart Jr.," she let me know.

The whole time she talked to me, she avoided eye contact. From one woman to another, I swear I could just feel her pain just by looking at her. I quickly wrote down her name along with the kids' as I got her documentation in order.

"Okay, and will you need help with finding a job? If so, we have job fairs hosted here every first and third Wednesday of the month. If you're lucky, most times they will hire you right on the spot. I'm going to hand you this paperwork, so you can see everything that we offer here. If you head to the back, there is a mall, as we like to call it, but it's just clothes from newborn all the way up to a four ex, which is free of charge, but there is a maximum of four outfits per person. The clothes come in every Monday, and most times they're donated from families, Goodwill, and we're teamed up with a few of the local boutiques around the area, so they'll often bring in brand new clothes as well.

"We offer daycare or babysitting services, if you need someone to watch your kids while you work. There's a cafeteria in the back, bathrooms, laundry rooms, whatever you need to make this stay as comfortable as possible. For one year, me, my mom, my brother, and my little sister stayed in a shelter. I know it's probably not my place to say anything to you, but I just want you to know that it gets better. It really does," I said with sympathy in my voice as I handed her the paperwork.

She simply nodded as she gathered her things along with her kids' things.

Off in the distance, I saw that a lot of the women standing in the line were looking at something. I wanted to know what had everyone's attention, but when I looked up, I saw my brother walking in. I playfully rolled my eyes because I swear these women were bat shit crazy when it came to my little brother. I'll be the first to admit that I had a very handsome brother, but even Omari Hardwick couldn't have me acting like this over him, and that was one fine ass man.

I was used to women crushing over my little brother, though. When I was in high school, I would literally have my friends telling me that they couldn't wait until my brother turned eighteen so that they could get with him. I would always tell them that they didn't stand a chance because at the time, he was with Amari, and she was all he cared about. The love that my brother had for Amari was so fuckin' beautiful. I've never in my life seen him love another woman as much as he loved Amari.

A part of Boss died when Amari died, so I knew that explained his new hobby of fuckin' all of these bird brain bitches. All I wanted was for my brother to get him one good woman and leave these bitches alone. I knew I got on his case a lot about being with different women, and I often said shit like his dick was going to fall off, but truth be told, I said all that shit because I was worried about him. I was worried that he would never slow down, and he was going to take the wrong woman home with him one day, and she was going to try and set my brother up.

He could say all he wanted about how he made the bitches give him their phone when they came over, but bitches were still spiteful and would find a way somehow. Anyway, Boss was so wrapped up in looking down at his phone, that he didn't even realize that mainly every woman in there was looking at him.

"Shit! My bad. My bad. I swear this fuckin' phone going to be the death of me. You alright?" Boss asked while bending down and picking up the bags that he'd just knocked out of the woman's hand who was just standing in my line with her two kids.

Winter was what she said her name was.

"Yes, I'm fine. Thank you," she said and took the bags from his hand.

I've literally watched women who came in contact with my brother act as if they were star struck, but it was so different to see a woman who didn't seem to be the least bit fazed by his looks. I laughed to myself because his cocky ass needed that. Now that he'd handed her back her bags, he stood there for a few seconds, just staring at her. I knew my brother; therefore, I knew that he wanted to say something, but he never got the chance because she grabbed her kids' hands and walked away.

"Who was that?" he asked, coming over to my line. His eyes weren't even on me. They were glued on Winter as she walked away.

"Really, Cortez? Get out the line so I can finish checking these people in," I told him, and he moved out of the way.

"Mama wanted me to come and sign over some paperwork. Find out who that is for me, though," he said, and just that fast, he'd walked away.

I paid my brother no mind because I could tell that that woman was already going through enough shit. I could tell that she was at a breaking point in her life, so hell no, I was going to put a word in and have him make her life more toxic than it already was; I didn't care if he was my brother or not.

CHAPTER ELEVEN

I drove all the way down to the center with food for my wife, only for her ass to tell me that she didn't want the food because she wasn't hungry. I hated it like a motha fucka that my wife knew me so much. I hated that I couldn't hide shit from her, because after eighteen years, she knew me like the back of her hand. Some shit happened during my trip to Los Angeles that I just didn't have the balls to come back and tell my wife, so yes, she wasn't tripping about the doubts that she had. Only thing is, her doubts were way off.

I hadn't messed around on Ocean in years, and I wasn't trying to backtrack, especially not when her crazy ass mama told me that she would burn down wherever I'm at with me in it if I broke her daughter's heart one more time. Early this morning, when Ocean sat on my lap, looked me deep in my eyes, and demanded the truth, I should have told her the truth then, but I couldn't. How the fuck was I supposed to tell her some shit like this when she still wasn't over the loss of our child?

She thought I didn't hear her because I didn't speak on it, but I heard her when she was in a separate room crying over the baby girl that we just lost a month ago. With the shit that I had to tell Ocean, I may as well get a gun and shoot her right in the chest with it because that's how this news was going to make her feel. I needed someone to talk this shit out with, so when Ocean declined the food that I'd brought to her, I sent Boss a text, telling him to meet me at one of my lounges in Miami.

I parked my Rolls Royce in my designated parking spot and went on inside. Because I was the owner of this bitch, I got treated like royalty. I walked right up in my own little section, and it wasn't long before one of my Hookah girls, (which my wife couldn't stand by the way) had come over and got everything ready for me to start smoking.

Ocean didn't like the women because they paraded around this bitch with little to nothing on, and she knew that they all wanted to fuck me. The shit that they wore kept niggas in and out this spot, and the more people, the more money that was transferred into my account. I'll be the first to admit that my cheating ways had caused my wife to be insecure like a motha fucka. In a way, I felt like I'd damaged her for good, even though I hadn't fucked around on her since I said I do.

Ocean was easily the prettiest woman I knew, but cheat on your woman with a bitch who doesn't have something that your wife has, and that'll break the baddest bitch. Ocean was tall with a slim build, so if I went out and fucked a thick broad, it was always, "Am I not thick enough for you?" Let me fuck a short bitch, and it was, "Am I too tall for you?"

To me, Ocean was perfect, but it was my imperfections that had me being a dog to her. My ole girl went through the same shit with my ole boy, and that's who my ole girl says that I get it from. Growing up, it was me and both parents, but most times, it was always just me and my ole girl because my ole boy was always fuckin' around, so he would always end up getting his ass kicked out. It wasn't that Ocean lacked anything, but I got with ocean at seventeen years old, so in a way, I felt like I'd been fuckin' married since a teenager.

My dumb ass just wanted to go through that phase of fuckin' on new bitches because I thought that new pussy would make the sex better, but I almost fucked around and lost my girl for good. I don't care how much new pussy is out there, that shit will never compare to the pussy that you have at home waiting for you. The pussy that's loyal, that no pulling out or no rubber pussy, and that pussy that'll have your ass smitten. It took me years to become this way, though. I wasn't always this loyal.

Now that my hookah was ready, I pulled it to my lips

and took a few shots. I liked to smoke my hookah with weed because it relaxed me, so that's exactly what I was doing. In a few more minutes, I spotted Boss walking through the door and nodded my head once his eyes landed on me. He frequented here a lot, and everyone knew this was my man, so the moment he came into my section, it wasn't long before a hookah was coming his way.

"Fuck you got going on, nigga, that you needed to see me ASAP? You lucky you my brother and that I was already in the area because anybody else would have had to wait," he told me after he'd reached his hand in and given me a pound.

I took a few pulls from the hookah before I released a sigh and pulled down on the beard that was growing thick as hell these days.

"I found some shit out when I went to L.A this weekend. Some shit that'll probably damage me and your sister for good, and—"

"Yoooo, I don't want to hear no more. Last time you did some dirt behind Ocean's back and she found out that I knew about it, she stopped talking to me for a whole fuckin' month. Whatever it was that you were about to say, keep that shit to yourself, nigga. I don't want to be involved in you and Ocean's shit. Fuck no," he said, and then he took a pull from his hookah as well.

"You don't even want to know some of it?" I asked him, and he quickly shook his head.

"No, because if you tell me that you were fuckin' around on my sister, I'm going to forget that we're supposed to be brothers, and I may just crack you upside your head with this fuckin' vase. Then we going to be in this bitch fighting. Yo, my sister just lost your baby a month ago. Does that not mean anything to you, man? You were in the room when the doctor told her that if she can even get pregnant again, any pregnancy for her will be high risk, so no, keep that shit," he said.

"You don't gotta fuckin' remind me that she just lost our baby. I was there when it fuckin' happened. She was lying in my damn arms when she started losing all that fuckin' blood. If you think that I would fuck around on your sister, especially at a time like this, then you obviously don't know me," I voiced.

It was nothing new for Boss and me to go toe to toe with each other. We both had very demanding, no bullshit attitudes that would sometimes lead to us throwing our shirts off and fighting like we were street fighters or some shit.

"I hear you, but still, leave me out of that shit. If you hiding something from Ocean, you better tell her now. Ya'll done been through too much shit for you to be keeping secrets from her," he told me, and I nodded.

We talked for about thirty more minutes until he headed out saying something about how he was having a meeting in another hour at one of his offices. Now that it was just me, I had plenty of time alone with my thoughts. With the job I had, it caused me to engage in social media a lot, although I didn't too much care for the shit. The moment I landed in LA, I posted it in my story, and I received a DM from someone who I was familiar with. Very familiar with for that matter. Her name was Tiana.

Tiana was the woman who I would fuck around with whenever Ocean and I were on a break. When Ocean would put a nigga out, instead of getting a hotel, I would crash at Tiana's spot. Most times, I would stay there until Ocean said that I could come back. That went on a lot, especially in my early-middle twenties because that's when I was a hot head.

When Ocean and I would be on a break, but mainly her taking a break from me because I never took a break from her, it would cause me to indulge in my fair share of drugs, such as weed, Xanax, and I was even sipping lean at one point. So yes, there were times when I would slide inside Tiana, and to this day, I cannot remember if I'd strapped up or not. When Ocean and I got married, which is when I was twenty-seven, it was as if Tiana had just disappeared off the face of the fuckin' earth, so when she DM'd me when I landed, I was shocked to see the message.

She was following me, but I wasn't following her, and because her profile was on private, all I could see was her profile picture, which was of her and a little girl who looked to be at least nine or ten. The message was her letting me know that she needed to talk. She made it known that she didn't want to fuck me; she had respect for the fact that I was married, and that she just wanted to talk.

All signs were telling me not to go, but my inquiring mind just wanted to know what she had to talk to me about. I knew that I should have just stayed my ass in my hotel room, but after attending all the meetings that I needed to attend for the day, I ended up meeting her at Starbucks. She looked exactly how she looked when I left her. That ass was still fat, and her waist was still tiny as hell.

Tiana had a dark brown skin complexion with jet black dreads like me that reached the middle of her back. Light brown eyes, a little hood in her, which was just how I liked my women, and she was classy. I hated to say this shit, and I'd never say it to my wife, but the two of them had a lot in common. Of course, they knew about each other. Well, Tiana had always known about Ocean, but Ocean didn't find out about Tiana until I aired out all my dirty laundry before we got married. We agreed to tell each other everything, so we wouldn't go into the marriage with secrets.

Do you know that I confessed damn near every woman that I fucked to my wife? In return, she told me that she didn't fuck anyone, but it was one guy who she was going to mess around with just to get some get back on me. On everything I love, the thought of my wife fuckin' a nigga almost made my ass cry. No one had been inside that pussy but me, so to hear her say that another nigga almost came close was similar to her telling me that she'd fucked someone.

So, when I met up with Tiana a few days ago, I didn't even get to take a sip from my drink before she laid the pictures of a ten-year-old little girl on the table who looked exactly like the picture of me that my ole girl still had hanging up in her living room. When I saw that picture, I swear to God a tear fell from my eye because I immediately thought of my wife and how this shit was going to hurt her.

Want to know some more fucked up shit about this whole situation? She named that little girl Neona, which she knew was the name that I said I wanted to name my daughter if I ever had one.

I was high one night and running off at the mouth, so that's how she knew to go with that name. Fucked up thing is, Ocean and I had paid to find out the gender when she was only ten weeks pregnant, and once we found out that she was pregnant with a little girl, we instantly said that we were going to name the baby Neona. So, not only did I now have a little girl, but I also had a little girl with the name that my wife adored. How the fuck was I supposed to tell my wife some shit like this? How?

She was questioning if she can ever even have children, and now I'm supposed to bring this shit on her? It had literally just been a month since the miscarriage, so I couldn't tell her this shit yet. I couldn't even be an asshole and tell Tiana that I wanted a DNA test because that little girl was my twin. What I did want to know was why wasn't I given the chance to know, and when I did ask her that, her response was that she knew I would tell her to get an abortion. Plus, when she found out that she was pregnant, I had already gone back to Ocean and proposed.

You know, I couldn't even be mad at Tiana as much as I wanted to be because this was all my doing. When them old heads preached about keeping your dick in your pants, this was why. There was no doubt in my mind that this was going to end my marriage. It didn't matter that the little girl was ten and that I impregnated Tiana while Ocean and I were on a break. My wife wouldn't want to hear those type of details. The only thing that would register in her mind was that I slipped up, and because of my slip up, I was now a father to a child that she didn't birth.

Tiana had even asked me if I wanted to come and meet her, but I quickly declined her offer. What I did do though, was Cash app her $10,000 dollars for her because I just didn't know what I wanted to do yet. Although my ole boy was one cheating ass nigga, he was one hell of a father, so I had to take that trait from him as well. I chose my wife in literally everything that I did, but if it came down to it, and she made me choose, I'm sorry but it would be my daughter. She was innocent in this shit and didn't ask to be here.

You could call me whatever fucked up name you wanted to call me, but I didn't want anyone calling me a dead beat. I learned from Tiana that when she found out that she was pregnant ten years ago, she moved to L.A because this was where her sister was. She ended up moving in with her, and she started dancing. So, there it is, I have a stripper for a baby mama, a daughter named after the daughter that my wife and I were supposed to have, and the moment that my wife found out all this shit, I was going to lose the one woman that I loved more than anything in this fuckin' world.

In the middle of the hookah lounge, pulling from this hookah that was on the way of getting me fucked up, a lone tear fell from my eye that I didn't even bother to wipe. Any other time in the past, I would have confidence that my wife would come back to me once everything calmed down, but deep down inside, with everything in me, I knew that this was it. Whenever the fuck I decided to tell my wife this shit, everything we had would be a thing of the past.

The last time I cheated, I told Ocean that if I break her heart again, she could just walk away because I felt like she deserved better. Here I was, breaking her heart yet again, and because I was a man of my word, I guess I would have to let her walk.

CHAPTER TWELVE

"It's a beautiful day out here today. We should sit outside this morning and have brunch," my mother said as she and I walked into Grand Lux Café this morning.

It was Saturday morning, and typically, every Saturday, my mom and I would meet up to have brunch somewhere. Truthfully, my mother and I were best friends, damn near sisters because we had such a tight bond and a loving relationship. I was an only child, so growing up, that allowed her to put all her time and attention into me, which is one of the causes of our tight relationship. I had my father in my life, but he and my mother divorced when I was six.

After the divorce, he moved to Michigan, where he now

had a family of his own, which had gained me two little sisters, but I didn't have a close relationship with them because I didn't necessarily have a close relationship with my father. I guess you can say that I resented him in a lot of ways. I was twenty-four years old and still holding onto old grudges from childhood. I've announced to my mother and him on a few occasions that when he divorced my mother, it kind of felt like he'd divorced me well.

During the first year of their divorce, he would always fly down for major holidays like Thanksgiving, Christmas, and he would even come down for my birthday. It wasn't until he re-married that our relationship started to fade, and he started mailing me things instead of just showing up. Christmas gifts were mailed along with birthday gifts. By the time I was sixteen, I just stopped caring altogether. It used to sadden me that I was no longer a "daddy's girl" like a lot of my good friends were, and that he'd stopped putting in effort, but these days, I just didn't give a fuck because I figured that it was his loss. Plus, I was older, and I knew the truth on why him and my mother divorced, so I definitely didn't care to have any type of relationship with him now.

I found out from my mother that for the last two years of their marriage, he was cheating on her with the woman that he's married to right now. In fact, one of the daughters that he had with her was a child that was conceived while he was still married to my mother. As you can see, a lot of drama that takes place in this big family, and somehow, I'm always somewhere right in the middle of it. Like, this whole damn situation that I'm in the middle of between my cousin, Camila, and Winter.

Let me explain my side of the story because I just hate to come off like the bad guy here. I'll be the first to say that although Dewayne is a few years older than me, he and I are very close. It didn't even feel like we were cousins because we had the bond of brother and sister. Dewayne's mother is sisters with my mother. The two of them are tight, and growing up, they spent a lot of time together, which caused Dewayne and I to be together all the time.

I always had a lot of friends growing up, and my cousin was handsome and could basically get any girl he wanted, so it wasn't out of the ordinary for him to ask me to set something up between him and one of my friends. When it came to his relationships, somehow, I was always in the middle of that shit. Now, his wife, Camila, that was his doing. He'd managed to get with her all on his own. In fact, I didn't meet her until the two of them had gotten serious and he started bringing her around the family.

For as long as I could remember, my cousin had always been a player. He was a pretty boy with a smooth talk about him, so it didn't take much for him to get with girls. Back in his teenage years, he went through his fair share of getting bullied by boys at the school because half of the time, he would take boys' girlfriends from them. Another thing that he was bullied on was his physical appearance. Now, my cousin was straight, but a lot of boys at school thought he was gay, simply because he was a pretty boy.

I remember his senior year in high school, he ended up

missing school for two weeks straight because there had been rumors around the school that he was caught in the bathroom with another guy. Crazy thing is, when he and I talked about it, he never admitted to doing it, nor did he admit to not doing it. I'd seen my cousin parade around with plenty of women, so I didn't think he was gay, but although I didn't think he was, that didn't take away from me feeling like he was attracted to men. I'll explain why I felt this way later.

He wasn't your typical manly man who would go out in the sun and play a sport, neither did he watch sports a lot for that matter. Dewayne would often accompany me to the nail salon whenever I went, and like the pretty boy he was, he would always get his manicure and his pedicure every three weeks.

I never saw anything wrong with his lifestyle. I just assumed that he was one of those men who liked to pamper himself, which I didn't see anything wrong with at all. I loved a man who would go out and get himself pampered because I hated talking to a guy with dirty fingernails, dirty ears, or anything dirty on their body for that matter. Dewayne having an interest in making sure that he kept himself up to par was never one of those things that had me questioning him.

I started having my doubts about Dewayne when the rumor came out in high school about him being in the bathroom with another guy. The guy that he was caught in the bathroom with, his name was Leon, and everyone around the school knew that Leon was gay. The thing is, Leon was fine as hell. Me and all the other girls hated that he was gay because we all wanted to have a chance with him. He wasn't the type of gay boy who wore dresses or anything. He just wore his school uniform pants a little tight, he had damn near every name brand purse because his mother was in the music industry at the time, so he was always dressed to the nines. In fact, he was pushing a beautiful BMW to school his senior year.

There was no doubt in my mind that Leon could get with any man who had the same sexual preference as him because he was just that handsome, which was why I didn't see the need for him to have to lie on my cousin. I never said it out of my mouth because my loyalty was with Dewayne, and I didn't want him to think that I was agreeing with everybody else who was calling him gay. I've caught my cousin on plenty of occasions looking at other men, and when he would catch me looking, he would always lie and say that he was just looking at his shoes or the sweater that the man had on was hard.

That was all I had. I never witnessed him with another man or anything. Any thoughts that I may have had about him being gay went out of my mind the moment he married Camila. The doubts left because if he were gay, why would he ask a woman to marry him and announce in a room full of people the day that they got married that he wanted to spend the rest of his life with her? When Camila and Dewayne married, he and I weren't as close as we used to be, simply because he was now a husband, and not too long after that, he'd become a father.

Winter didn't come into the picture until like the fourth year of their marriage. I don't know what the hell was going on with my cousin and Camila at that time, but all I know is that Camila had gone back home to her country for a few months. From pieces of information that Dewayne told me, she was feeling neglected by him because he was never home anymore, so she'd left to be around her family because majority of her family was in Columbia.

During the time that she spent away, is when Dewayne met Winter. Now, I don't know if any of this shit is true; I'm just simply stating what my cousin told me. He admitted out of his own mouth that Winter was just supposed to be a quick fuck and something for him to entertain while his wife was away. I called that bullshit the moment it left his mouth because if that was the case, he never would have proposed, neither would he have gone and purchased that big ass house for the two of them.

Now, when it came to the kids that Dewayne had with Winter, he told me that he was giving her hints to make her get an abortion, but she just wouldn't take the hints. Then, as far as the proposal goes, he said that the only reason he proposed was to shut her up. He told me something about how Winter started questioning him about meeting more people in his family, so the ring was just to stall her on all the questions. The only reason I knew these things is because Dewayne would tell me. He would tell me because he felt horrible about what he had done to Winter. He played the fuck out of this woman's heart, left her with two children, and was married the whole time.

When I said little things to Winter over the years like, "Are you sure this marriage is going to happen?" I swear to God that I was trying to put bugs in her ear, but her head was so far stuck up Dewayne's ass that she couldn't even take the hints that I was throwing.

She took it as me being jealous, but little did she know that although Dewayne was my cousin, I would never in my life want a man like him. He doesn't know how to love women. He thinks that love is giving his women money, a new car, or fancy things that ordinary people couldn't afford, which was the furthest thing from love. Should I have been a woman and told Camila the truth about my cousin and Winter? Hell no, because Dewayne is my blood, and I would never throw him under the bus like that. It wasn't my place to tell then, and with him dead, it still wasn't my place to say shit. This was one of those things that I was going to let die with me.

With Camila in Columbia and Winter wherever the hell she was staying at now, hopefully this whole thing would just blow over, and this conversation will be in the past.

"Yeah, we can sit outside. I don't mind," I finally responded to my mother, now that we were standing up front facing the hostess.

My mother notified her that we wanted to sit outside, and it wasn't long before she had two menus in her hands, and she was walking us to the shaded area outside that had a nice breeze that wasn't too strong or too light. The moment our waiter came over, my mom and I both ordered a mimosa while we read over the menu to see what we wanted to order for brunch.

"I forgot to tell you that Julius called me yesterday," my mom said set the menu down after she'd finished looking it over.

Julius was pretty much the family lawyer. He was Dewayne's lawyer first, but because he'd done such a great job with Dewayne, everyone in the family had pretty much hired him. I guess you can say that the Stewart family was a very wealthy family, so Julius came in handy a lot.

"Oh yeah? What did he want?" I asked, closing the menu because I knew what I wanted as well.

"I guess he couldn't get in contact with my sister, so he called me. He told me that Camila called him a few days ago, and she told him that she would be in town next weekend and she wanted to schedule an appointment with him because she had a few questions that she wanted to get answered. She wouldn't tell him much on the phone about what it was that she wanted to talk about either. I'm assuming that it has something to do with money. Let's be real, that girl only got with Dewayne because of his wealth," my mom said right before she rolled her eyes.

I've always thought that, but I never said it out of my own mouth. Hell, I didn't even think my mom felt that way, so when she said it, I laughed a little bit. My mother was just as messy as I was, if not worse.

"I have my reasons for thinking that, but why do you think that?" I inquired because I genuinely wanted to know why she felt that way.

"Please! It's obvious! I remember when Dewayne brought her around the first time. Everybody was throwing question after question her way, and I remember asking her if she wanted kids. She said hell no! Notice how when Dewayne started expanding his businesses more and more that she finally started pushing out kids for his ass. I never liked her. I always made that clear. It was always something about her that screamed gold digger and money hungry," my mom voiced to me, and I nodded because I agreed with her to a certain extent.

I didn't necessarily think that Camila was with Dewayne strictly for his money because she came into the relationship with money of her own, just not as much money as my cousin. After my mom finished speaking, the waiter came back over with our drinks, and he finally took our order. The moment he disappeared, I could feel my mom's eyes on me, so I looked up at her. From that look, I could tell that the conversation was going to switch gears and that she was going to all of a sudden get serious with me.

"Yes, I wanted to meet with you this morning for our usual girl's day, but I also wanted to let you know that I don't believe you when you say that you don't know this Winter chick. I would have come to you sooner about this, but losing Dewayne felt like I'd lost a son more than losing a nephew because you know how close he and I were. That woman came to the hospital that night looking especially for you. You claim to not have known how she knew to come to the hospital, but I think you forgot that while everyone was in the family room that night at the hospital, you disappeared for at least ten minutes. I'm smart enough to know that during that time, your ass called her.

"I was married to your father for almost ten years, and he was the president of lying ass niggas, and I hate to say this, but you take after him in that department. So, as your mother, I want to know the truth. Do you know that woman or not?" she firmly asked me.

I thought about her question long and hard. I didn't lie to my mother, but I would damn sure keep secrets from her. I thought about if I had anything to lose if I were to tell her all these things and the only thing that I was really losing was my cousin's trust, but that wasn't really worth much because he was gone, so it really wasn't like I needed it. It took about a minute for me to start speaking, and when I did, it was like I all of a sudden got diarrhea of the mouth. I swear that I told it all and, in the end, I felt like I could breathe again because I'd been holding onto this shit for years, never telling anyone what I really knew. In a way, it kind of felt like a weight had been lifted off my shoulders.

"Wow, you are definitely your father's child. You really stood your ass there that night and pretended not to know that woman and her kids. Made me and everyone in that room think that woman was delusional or some shit. Juju, you got to know that that shit is hateful as fuck. For you to have known the history and the extent of the relationship that she had with Dewayne and to pretend not to have known shit is foul. You don't do people like that," my mom said, and I could hear it in her voice that she was very disappointed in me.

"Ma, what the hell did you want me to do? Look disloyal in front of the whole family since I knew what was going on this whole time? Dewayne didn't love Winter the way that he loved Camila, so it was more important for me to protect his wife while at the same time protecting my cousin, even in his death! Winter had to have known something, Ma, so I honestly don't feel too bad for her. Ma, Dewayne would spend weeks at a time away from her, lying to her and telling her that he was out of town on business, whole time he was a mile away with his real family. She should have known," I said, and she simply shook her head right before she took a sip of her drink.

"Just like I should have known that your father was cheating on me with a whole other family in Michigan, right? My dear child, love will blind you. I was deeply in love with your father, so when your father told me that he was taking care of business, my silly ass believed him. As women, we tend to love hard, and we never want to accept the fact that our man just may be doing some foul shit behind our backs, but that doesn't make us dumb. I sympathize with Winter because I was that woman before. I know how it feels to be lied to, cheated on, and embarrassed in front of everybody. You just pray to God that you never meet a man and God decides to have that man put karma on you. You claim to hate your daddy so much for what he did to me, yet you love your cousin so much for what he did to both his wife and to Winter. Think about that," she said.

I heard everything she said. Maybe I was blind to it right now because I just didn't see what I did that was so wrong. I wasn't friends with either Winter or Camila. I tolerated them due to the relationships that they had with my cousin, and if that made me a bad person, then so be it. I know that if the shoe was on the other foot and I wanted my cousin to have my back in something like this, that he would have done the same thing for me in return.

CHAPTER THIRTEEN

ONE MONTH LATER

It was two in the morning. Instead of lying in the bed with my children, I was outside on the step at the center with my back against the wall, my feet pulled into my chest, and damn near on the verge of tears. I didn't know what the hell I was expecting to happen, but it's been a whole month, and I'm still living in this shelter with my children. Don't get me wrong, this place was very accommodating, and I would choose this over living with Sandra any day, but I just wanted to give more to my children, you know? They were so little that they thought that this was just a big sleepover with other adults and children, so they loved it here.

The shelter had a little playground area outside that my kids loved to go and bond with other little kids their age. I usually let them go out there for an hour before we would get on the bus for me to drop them off at Anita's house before I went to work. Anita knew about our living arrangements and had damn near begged me to move into her apartment with my kids, but I just couldn't. Hell, I wouldn't! I wanted to have some type of pride left. Not only that, but she had a grown man living in the house with her, which was her son. I was protective of my babies and didn't want them to live under the same roof with a man like that.

When I was younger, I used to eavesdrop on Sandra's conversations when she would be in the living room with her girlfriends catching them up on the latest gossip. I remember one time listening to her conversation, and I heard her mention something about one of the little girls in the neighborhood getting raped by their mother's boyfriend. So, the fear of having my children around other men had been something that had stuck with me ever since I heard Sandra say that.

I know you may be wondering why I would leave my children at Anita's house while I went to work, and the answer to that question is because I knew that Anita would have my kids in the room with her while I was away, and I knew that she would never leave my children alone with her son. I remember expressing to her that if she ever had to leave to let me know because I would walk out in the middle of my job to come and get my babies. She didn't take offense to my feelings, but in the same breath, she did let it be known that her son was harmless and wouldn't do anything to harm my kids.

Aside from me not wanting to have my kids laid up in the same house as Anita's son, Sandra would often drop by Anita's house, and I just didn't want her to have the satisfaction of seeing me sleeping on her best friend's couch. While I was living at the shelter, I could have a little bit of pride because I knew that Sandra wouldn't be caught dead at a shelter. Nights like this, as I sat outside, still in my work clothes, I thought about life and everything that I'd been through that had led me to this moment.

The only memories that I had of Dewayne were in my head and my children. I hated him. I hated him for doing this to us and our children. We didn't mean a damn thing to him. It was basically like he put it in his will for me and the kids to struggle when he died because that's exactly what the hell took place. For him to think that it was okay in that sick head of his to take everything away from us had me wishing that he would burn in hell. My thing is, he didn't have to include me in shit, but what about his children? He could have left something behind for them for when they turned eighteen, but I guess the only children that really mattered to him were the ones he shared with his wife.

In the matter of four months, I'd gone from loving the hell out of this man to hating him. I would say that I wish I never met him, but then I wouldn't have the twins, and Lord knows that that little boy and girl are my peace. They are the reason why I still have my sanity right now. When they got old enough and could fully understand the things that I tell them and not just let it go in one ear and out of the other, I swear that I was going to teach them some shit about life. I was going to instill values in them about being independent and making smart decisions.

I'll teach them both the same qualities, but I swear I'm going to go just a little bit harder on my daughter. I'll teach her the things that Sandra never taught me, so she never has to be lost in this world all because she fell victim and weak for a man and allowed him to have her forgetting about her worth and her value. Like I said before, I never thought that this day would happen, so I never prepared for this. I will admit that ignorance and my ability to be gullible and naïve is what landed me here, but I can bet my last dollar that I will never allow another man to make a fool out of me like this.

I was pretty close with the woman who bunks with me, so while I sat out here with my thoughts, she was inside watching over my kids because, just like me, it was hard for her to sleep these days. Her name is Teagan, and she has a beautiful, four-year-old daughter, named Meagan. I like Teagan a lot, but Lord knows I didn't want my story to be similar to hers.

Next month will mark a year that she's been in here. Just like the man I was with wasn't shit, Teagan's man wasn't shit either. Only difference was that he was physical abusive in the relationship that she was in with him. This shelter was pretty much her hiding spot away from him with her daughter. At nights like this, usually she and I would stay up and we engage in conversation about our past. I can honestly say that whenever she talked about the physical abuse that she endured from her husband, the hairs on my back would stand up, and I would find myself getting emotional because she dealt with that shit from him for years.

She was telling me the other day that the night she escaped, he'd come home late from the bar, and not only was he trying to attack Teagan, but he was going for their daughter as well. She said that she ran and never looked back. Although at night I prayed for myself and my kids religiously, I also prayed that Teagan's ex didn't find her because he was a monster, and it scared me what he would do to her if he ever caught up with her. She even told me out of her own mouth that there is no doubt in her mind that he would kill her if he caught her, and for that, I feared for her.

While I worked at Walmart, she worked at Costco during the day. She and I were putting our paychecks to the side with hopes of getting out of here in a few months and getting an apartment together for ourselves and our kids. Funny how we hadn't known each other for long, but when we talked, it felt like I'd known her for years. We were just able to relate on so much stuff. From feeling isolated as a child to having a mother who didn't give a fuck about us, and then growing up and finding love all in the wrong person.

I hated that all the things we had in common were of

elements of a struggle, but damn did it feel good to know that I wasn't the only one going through this shit.

About five minutes had passed when all of a sudden, a big, 20 foot U-Haul truck pulled up in the front of the center. Whoever the hell was driving that truck couldn't have possibly had their driver's license because as they were backing the truck in, I really thought for a second that they were going to back into the building. I was even almost prepared to get up just in case they did.

"Yoooo! Your ass can't fuckin' drive for shit! On the way back, I'm driving this shit back before you fuck around and kill me," I heard a deep, even sexy voice say, and followed by that was the passenger side door slamming.

I didn't know who the voice belonged to because I could only see the figure from the back. If his back was this attractive, I could only imagine what his front looked like. You have to excuse me because I haven't been touched by a man in damn near one whole year. He wore a black fitted wife beater that clung to his body and showed off the well-defined muscles that he had in his back. He had on black joggers that hung off his waist a little bit, just enough for you to see the emblem for whatever kind of boxers he wore.

I couldn't stand a man who sagged his pants, especially when they had their whole ass out, but the way his pants hung was perfect. Sneakers were on his feet, and when he turned around, I immediately knew who he was. How the hell could I have forgotten that face? Whoever the driver was, they said something back to him that I couldn't make out. Whatever was said it made him laugh, and I could have died when he laughed and showed off those perfect dimples.

In the wifebeater that he wore, I could see the big shoulder tattoo that was on his body, making his arm look sexier than it already was. His hair was cut to perfection, and I could tell that he took his time when he brushed it, making sure it would give him the most perfect waves possible. A long, full beard, that would probably tickle the hell out of you if you were to lean in and kiss him. There was no doubt about it that this man was beautiful. My God, why could I see his dick print all the way from over here? I had perfect vision, so I was very aware of what I saw.

I knew that I would never in my life get a guy who looked even half as good as he did, so I removed my eyes from him and kept looking off into space, like I was originally doing before they pulled up. It was getting late, so in a few more minutes, I was going to head back inside anyway\s. I could use a hot shower and some much-needed sleep.

"You can't possibly be from around here, because if so, you would be inside that building buried under the covers. It's not safe on this side of town, shorty, you may want to get inside," one of the dudes said.

This one had a high yellow skin tone and long dreads. He was handsome as well, but I liked the one in the all-black. Let me rephrase that because I didn't know him well enough to like him. I just felt like the one in the all-black could just simply look at you, and boom, you're pregnant. I remembered when he'd bumped into me a month ago and the intoxicating cologne that he had on that day. Of course, I chose to not get flattered when he talked to me because I knew that he was wayyyy out of my league. I wondered what the women looked like that he dated because they for damn sure didn't look like me.

If anything, I chose to make our conversation quick and simple because, for goodness sake, I was checking into a shelter with my kids, so that man wouldn't want a damn thing with me.

"I'm good. I know how to protect myself," I called out to him, and he laughed.

"Boss, shorty said she knows how to protect herself. Tell her about this part of town," the one with the dreads said again.

If only he knew the part of Miami I grew up in, he would just save his breath. Shoot outs and drivebys were the norm. This part of town was damn near equivalent to the middle and upper class to me because it wasn't as bad as what I was accustomed to.

"Nigga, this why my sister always cursing your ass out every other day of the fuckin' week. Your ass too fuckin' friendly. You always going around making friends with people. Be more like me. I'm one antisocial motha fucka and—"

All of a sudden, his voice stopped once he saw that it was me his friend was talking to. I looked back at him, wondering if his name was Boss for real. God, he was so handsome! He'd just climbed back into the truck after removing three boxes off the back and placing it on the ground. He was looking at me in a way that I could tell he was trying to remember where he knew me from. See, my face wasn't even that memorable. We'd just seen each other a month ago! He spoke to me and everything.

I had to laugh at myself because I was really about to get upset about the fact that this man didn't know who I was. Feeling like I'd been out there for too long, I stood up from the step that I was sitting on, used my hands to wipe off the back of my pants, and turned to head inside.

"Wait. Hold up for a second" I heard his deep voice say before he jumped down from the truck and jogged over to me.

"And you calling me friendly! Look at your ass. Don't be taking all night, Boss, because I know you going to try and be slick and have me tote all this shit out of this truck by my damn self. Your sister gave me an hour max to be out, and if I come home a minute later, she going to be doing what she do best, bitching," his friend said, and I had to laugh.

The two of them had been going at it since they parked the truck a few minutes ago. God, I would like to have been a fly in that truck on their way over here because I could only imagine the off the wall things that they had been saying to each other on the drive over. The one coming my way, whose name I thought was Boss, all he did was wave off his friend. As soon as he was close to me, I could smell a mixture of weed and that same cologne that he had a month back. He was so damn tall that when he was standing directly in front of me, I had to look up at him. I wasn't even short; I was an average height of about 5'5".

"I remember you from when you were checking in. How you liking it so far?" he asked.

"There's nothing like having your own home, but this is great as opposed to having to live on the streets. My kids love it. To them, it's just one big sleepover," I let him know.

There was that laugh again and those damn dimples.

"My ole girl actually owns this place. We used to stay in shelters growing up, but they were nowhere near as accommodating as this one. When it comes to single, struggling moms, that's just some shit that my ole girl has a big heart for, so she doesn't spare shit when it comes to these shelters. I guess because of the fact that she was once in a lot of the women shoes, she's able to sympathize with them or what not," he let me know.

"Wow, Ms. Brenda is your mother? I met her a couple days ago, and she's such a sweetheart. I ran into her in the cafeteria with my kids, and she did tell me a little bit about her story. I knew about her having three kids, but I didn't know that you were her son," I told him.

Crazy how I was standing there having a conversation like this with him because I was usually so quiet, shy, and reserved.

"Yeah, that's my ole girl. I do whatever I can to help out around here. Me and my boy over there, we pick up clothes from local thrift stores, but a night like tonight, we actually went into the malls and brought all types of clothes and shit for the kids and the parents. Somebody gotta cater to their needs, right?" he asked me, and I nodded.

The fact that him and his friend had brought all of these

clothes for the shelter had me looking at him like he was more attractive than I previously thought he was. I let him know that what he was doing was great, until I started to feel a little awkward. There wasn't anything else to really talk about, so I started slowly inching for the door.

"You didn't tell me your name," he called out behind me.

I turned around and I looked at him for a second.

"That's only because you didn't ask for it," I responded.

"What is it then? What's your name?" he asked.

"It's Winter."

"Winter. I like that. Winter what?"

I looked at him like he was crazy for inquiring on my last name. A laugh fell from his lips, and then he used his hand to pull down on his goatee. If I didn't know any better, I would think that I was making him nervous.

"I guess that did come off as me being a creep or some shit. What Walmart do you work at?" he asked, pointing to the uniform that I had on.

I was wearing a pair of khaki skinny leg bottoms with a blue polo shirt and the yellow cardigan with the Walmart logo on it.

"The one on 27th, by the stadium," I let him know.

"You like it?" he inquired.

I took a few seconds to think about his question before I just blurted out anything.

"These days, I don't think it's so much of what I like anymore. It's really just about what's going to help me be able to provide for my kids. The job itself, of course I don't like being on my feet all day, lifting heavy ass boxes, and stocking aisles and aisles of items, but I do it for my kids. I work long hours, which takes a lot of time away from me that I can be spending with my babies, but they understand that Mommy has to work," I said.

There was a long pause, and then he moved a few steps closer to me.

"You know how to work a computer?" he asked.

I laughed at his question, but when he didn't laugh back, I assumed that he was serious.

"Of course, I can work a computer," I let him know.

"With you working at Walmart, I'm assuming you have some type of customer service skills then, right?" he asked me.

"Yes, I'm pretty good when it comes to customer service. I'm around customers pretty much all day, so I have to be spot on when it comes to that," I said.

"You said you know how to work computers. Would you know how to go into Word and type up meeting notes? What about Excel? Do you know how to put together charts and shit?" he asked, and my eyes went up in confusion because I wondered why he was asking me all of those questions. "It's a yes or no question sweetheart. I'm trying to see if you fit the description for a job I have open," he said.

"I can type up a Word document. Although I don't know how to use Excel, I'm a fast learner, so if someone shows it to me, I know that I'll be able to do it," I told him.

"Would you be scared to talk in front of a room full of people? It can be anywhere from fifty to one hundred people at a time. You have a beautiful ass voice, but do you know how to use it? Can you conduct meetings, without having people look at you, like what the fuck are you talking about?" he asked, and with not a lot of confidence, I nodded my head up and down that I did.

I didn't know if conducting a meeting was my cup of tea. A few times in high school, I had to present my projects in front of the class, and I would like to think that I did pretty good with that. I was smart in school. I was that kid who would sit in the back of the classroom, never participated, but I would make straight A's. When I graduated from high school, it wasn't that I didn't want to go off to college, but it was more like I wanted to get a job quickly and make some easy money, so I could move out of Sandra's house.

I missed out on a lot of things throughout my years of high school, especially my senior year. I didn't attend any homecomings, grad bash, prom, nothing. I was surprised that I even went to my graduation. Anita and my sister, Summer, were the only two people who showed up to my graduation, but that was more than enough people for me. Sandra supposedly had to work the night of my graduation, which was why she didn't come.

"Okay, let's say I'm an investor, right? I'm looking into investing my money into this shelter. I want to get new beds for the mothers and the kids. I would like to remodel the bathrooms, the cafeteria area, and even the playground. Convince me why I should invest in this shelter and not the one that's down the street. I'm giving you sixty seconds to convince the fuck out of me," he said and folded his arms across his chest while looking me dead in my eyes as if she was waiting for me to begin talking.

When he looked at his Apple watch and pressed something on it then showed me the time, I saw that the sixty seconds had started, so I began talking.

"This is the Women and Children's shelter. For the past five years, it's been voted the number one shelter here in Miami. It accommodates the needs of mothers and their children. What sets this facility apart from any other shelter is the fact that all the staff here treats the residents like human beings as opposed to other shelters that tend to treat their residents like burdens. I think you should invest in this property because with it continuing to be voted number one, it's going to draw in more people. With more people coming, we should want to show them the best of the best, even if that includes remodeling the bathrooms, cafeteria, or whatever else needs remodeling. Not only will you do a good deed for the company, but you'll do a good deed for yourself. You'll be able to look back and know that the money you invested into this building was appreciated, valued, and treasured—"

"Time!" He stopped me once the timer went off. Now that I was finished, I looked at him like, "Now what?" I wanted to know about this position that he was talking about.

If he'd just stood there and wasted my time, I swear I was going to be too upset. I would give two fucks about how fine he was either.

"I own different apartments, condos, and townhouse

complexes throughout Miami, Miramar, and Fort Lauderdale. My general manager at one of my Miami complexes just informed me this week that his wife received a job promotion in Chicago. They both decided that she should take the position, which puts me in a fucked-up position because I'm losing my top manger out of all of my businesses, and he's been with me for the past five years.

"Almost ten minutes ago, I asked you if you liked your job. You told me no and that you were just doing it because you had to provide for your children. That right there shows me that you have drive. It shows me that you're not lazy either. When I came to a shelter with my family years ago, I was hoping that some good shit happened for my ole girl where she would get her hands on some money and get us the fuck up out of there. I was doing my own little thing at the time, making a little bit of my own money, but my ole girl wouldn't take my dirty money.

"Once she finally got enough money for us, we were able to move into an apartment. I see you, and for some reason, I see how my ole girl was back in the day. I want to give you the chance that I was wishing that somebody would have given my ole girl years ago. Let me offer you the position of being the general manager at the Miami office. It's a starting salary of $80,000 dollars that comes with benefits and everything. It's a Monday-Friday job, with hours of 8:00-5:00 P.M.

"I will not stand here and lie to you that this is going to be an easy job. This shit is very demanding, and renting is a very competitive job, so there will be days that you might have to come into the office a little earlier than usual. They'll be times when you have to stay a little later, coming up with ways to make our company mission better than any other company mission that's in close proximity to us. I know you have two kids, but with this job, I think you'll be able to provide better for them than you already are. What you think, Winter?" he asked.

I was still on the part where he said that my salary was going to be $80,000 dollars. I could feel my eyes beginning to water because if he was serious, then God had really answered my prayers and gone above and beyond what I had been praying for.

"Are you serious right now?" I asked him as I used the back of my hands to wipe away the happy tears that had fall from my eyes.

I mean, when I saw him a month ago dressed up in his fancy suit, I assumed he had a good job, but I didn't think he had this good of a career.

"You got kids, shorty. I wouldn't play about some shit like that. The moment your kids were involved was the moment that this shit was serious to me," he said, and I wanted to wrap my arms around him, possibly jump on him, but I didn't.

I did thank him over ten times, though, because I was very appreciative, and I would be a fool to turn this offer down.

"Boss, you done made me unload all of this shit, so your black ass can definitely drive on the way back. I already told you that your crazy ass sister gave me an hour to be out. If you the reason why I gotta sleep in a different room tonight, we going to have some problems," his friend yelled at him.

We both laughed. I'd honestly forgotten that he was even there because for the first time since he's been there, he was actually quiet.

"You work tomorrow? I'm going to come back over to finish discussing the job with you, tell you a little bit more about the company, and shit like that," he let me know.

"I'm off on Sundays," I let him know and he nodded.

"Alright, I'll be over sometime in the afternoon then. Winter, I want you to know something before I walk away, though. I know that a lot of times women have this whole idea that men only do nice shit when they want something from a female. I know that because I have two sisters, and I've listened to some of the talks that my ole girl would have with them over the years. I want you to know that I don't want shit from you, shorty. I'm not looking to fuck you, you don't have to pay me back with nothing, because at the end of the day, if you do right on the job, it'll be you that's helping me and not the other way around. Remember that. Also, just think of your living arrangements right now as a thing of the past because pretty soon, you'll be out of here. I'll get up with you later, though," he said and just like that, he walked away.

He didn't even give me a chance to respond. I didn't know if I was crushing or if I was just so happy about the new job that I was offered, but like an idiot, I stayed outside and watched him as he jumped into the driver's seat of the truck, and it wasn't long before he was pulling out of the parking lot. For the first time in a long ass time, I walked inside the building with a big smile on my face.

Once I took my shower and everything, I climbed into my bunk, and just like every other night, it was hard for me to fall asleep. This time, I couldn't sleep for all the right reasons. It was the beginning of the month and I was thinking on how hopefully by the end of the month, myself, Teagan, Meagan, and my kids would be able to get the hell up out of there. Don't get me wrong, this place was very special to me, but nothing would beat the feeling more of actually having a real home to go to after the end of a long work day.

CHAPTER FOURTEEN

The plane had just landed back in Miami about an hour ago, and here I sat in the back of an Uber on my way to confront Julius. Flying down to Miami was the last thing that I wanted to do, especially when my baby boy was only four months old, and I didn't want to leave him back in Columbia with my family, but I had so many questions for Julius today.

Ever since I talked to him about a month back on the phone and I started questioning some of the details of my husband's death, he'd been avoiding all of my phone calls. I called him at least ten times throughout the day, and in return, he'd send me a text message, letting me know that he'll get back to me soon, but soon would never come, and I was sick and tired of waiting on his ass! Playing around with Julius, I would never get in contact with him, so I had to go with my gut feeling and jump on a plane this morning.

I planned to ambush him at his office and leave him with no choice but to answer the questions that I had. The fact that he didn't even know that I was coming was what made this whole thing ten times better because it didn't leave him with any time to come up with a lie, if there were in fact any lies that he was hiding from me. I had a few reservations about things that I was blind to months ago when my husband passed, but now that I was in a place where I could make it through a day without crying over the death of my husband, I wanted to address a few things about my husband's death that just wasn't making any sense to me.

This had nothing to do with me wanting any more money either because I had more than enough money. I had a savings account that was hefty when my husband was here, and best believe it's still hefty even in his absence. Not only that, but my husband left me more than enough money in his will, so this was nothing about my financial situation. In fact, it was actually deeper than that.

The Uber driver finally pulled the car in front of the building, and I made sure to thank him before I got out. All I had with me were the clothes on my back and the purse that was on my shoulder because if things went as planned today, I would be back on a plane in a few hours. I'd been preparing for this day for weeks now, so I had all the questions that I planned to ask Julius stored in my head.

I walked into the building, and the first person I saw was

a receptionist. She looked to be in her middle twenties and was sitting at the desk, texting away on her phone, which I doubt she was supposed to be doing. The moment she heard the door chime, and she saw me, she quickly put the phone away.

"Hello. How may I help you?" she kindly asked me.

"I'm here to see Julius Grant. Is he in today?" I asked.

"Last I checked, he was. I'll give him a call and see. What's your name, by the way?" she asked.

"It's a surprise. I just flew in from Colombia, and I'm trying to surprise him. Just know that he's a friend of my family. We go way back," I let her know.

She smiled while nodding her head and picking up the work phone that was in front of her. She pressed a few buttons on the phone, and I watched her as she waited.

"Mr. Grant. There's a woman out here in the lobby, waiting to see you. Can I go ahead and send her back?" she asked.

From the look on her face, I could tell that she was deeply listening to whatever he was saying. If only I could hear what he was saying to her in response. She finally removed the phone from the mouthpiece and looked at me.

"He says that your going to have to tell me who you are, so that I can send you on back. He doesn't feel like being surprised right now. Plus, he says that there are only a handful of people in his life that he's associated with, so not many people can come and surprise him," she let me know and I rolled my eyes.

"Tell him it's Mrs. Stewart," I said, and she relayed the message.

Again, I could tell that she was deeply listening to what he was saying before she relayed the message to me.

"He's in a meeting, and after this, he says that he has to meet with a client. He said that you should have called first, that way you could have avoided the trouble of finding out that he's going to be busy all day and won't get a chance to speak with you. He wanted me to let you know that there are other lawyers here that you can speak with who—"

I reached over the desk and snatched the phone from her ear. I wasn't about to stand my ass there and play telephone with someone who I've been trying to get in contact for a whole month. If I didn't feel like he was bullshitting me before, I definitely felt like he was doing it now. The fact that he could be on the phone with her and continue to relay different messages to me proved that he wasn't in any damn meeting.

"Julius, I tried to have some type of respect for you by not just walking on back and bursting into your office because you know me. You know that I would do that. Out of respect for you being someone that my husband was very close with, I wanted to have respect for you and your job, but if you continue to make up excuses on why you cannot take a few minutes out of your day just to have a simple conversation with me, I will lose whatever respect I have left for you. Now, if you were smart, you would go ahead and give me the okay to come on back because even if I have to kick down your damn door, you will speak to me.

Now, which way would you prefer to do this?" I kindly asked him without raising my voice even once.

The fact that I was so calm about this entire thing is what should have had him shaking in his boots.

"Come on back, Mrs. Stewart," he calmly said.

With a smile on my face that showed my gratitude, I passed the receptionist back the phone and I headed on back. Once I neared his office, I could see him standing there with the door open waiting for my arrival. The whole time I walked to him, I was trying to read his facial expression, but it was damn near blank.

Julius was a nice guy for the most part, so it was kind of weird to see him and he not have that big, vibrant smile on his face that he always held. Because this was the furthest thing from a social call, I didn't even speak once I neared him. I just simply walked past him, and like I owned the place, I took a seat in his office.

It took him a few seconds, but he did eventually move away from the door to come inside and join me. He walked over to me and he took a seat on the opposite side, and I picked up on how hard it was for him to keep his eyes on me. The fact that he couldn't make complete eye contact with me was the first strike to me believing in that he was hiding something. Growing up, it was me, my mom, my dad, and my two sisters. Both my parents had instilled a lot of shit in me throughout my childhood, and my ability to smell bullshit from a mile away was similar to Floyd Mayweather in the boxing ring; meaning that I was a beast when it came to pinpointing someone's weak points.

"First things first, I would like to see my husband's death certificate because that was never shown to me," I said to Julius, with my hand against my chest and my leg crossed. My whole posture screamed that I meant business and that I didn't come all the way down here to play with his ass.

"Sure thing, Mrs. Stewart. If that was all you needed, I could have faxed that over to you and saved you the flight," he said, standing up from the chair that he was sitting in.

I watched as he walked over to a file cabinet, more than likely looking for the death certificate that I'd requested.

"Yes, because it's that easy to get on the phone with you," I sarcastically called back out to him. "This is nowhere near everything that I wanted, which is why I flew out here to get answers from you. I think your position in my life, with you not only being our lawyer, but also a friend, has caused you to get really comfortable in your position. If this is how you treat all your clients, then I'll be the first one to let you know that you are very unprofessional," I let him know.

"And I apologize for that," he said as he walked back over to me with a manila folder in his hands. "With all due respect to you, Mrs. Stewart, you and your family are not the only people that I service. I have about twenty clients on my back, and I wish I had the power to service you all at the same time, but it's just impossible for me to make something like that happen. Not to come off as rude, but when Mr. Stewart was alive, I always had to deal with him. When things needed to be taken care of or if he wanted to set up a meeting with me, he knew that because of my demanding lifestyle, that most times I wouldn't get back to him until the next day or even a couple of days, but the thing is, he was always able to understand that. With you having to step up and take his place, I'm assuming that this is all new for you. Here is the death certificate that you asked for," he finally said as he went back to the seat that he was previously sitting in and handed me the document.

I ignored everything he said because seeing this death certificate with my own eyes was most important to me right now. I had to have been staring at the certificate for at least five minutes, checking it out, just making sure that it was legit. The only other death certificate that I'd ever seen in my life was from my father when he passed away from cancer a few years ago. It was stamped, signed, and a certified copy, so I knew that this had to have been legit.

"I have a few other questions about the night of my husband's death. Who else besides you and the doctor saw his body? For months now, everything about that night has been sort of a blur to me. Slowly but surely, it's all coming back. I vividly remember you and the doctors damn near convincing me and the family that it was in our best interest to not go back and see him because it wasn't a way that we would want to remember him. Why were the two of you so against us seeing our loved one for the last time?" I asked the question that I had been wanting to know for quite some time now. I watched as Julius pulled down on his tie before he opened his mouth to answer my question.

"And if given the opportunity again, I would have done the same thing. Mrs. Stewart, you saw the condition of the vehicle that your husband was driving in that night. No disrespect, but how do you possibly think he would look after enduring an accident as awful as that one? I hate to say this, but there are times when I actually wish that I didn't go to the back and see the body because I cannot get that image out of my head.

"Every time you call me, it's kind of like you force me to relive that night and those images resurface, so in a way, I have been avoiding you, but it was only for my sanity. With every fiber in my body, I'm honestly telling you that you and your family are lucky that you didn't go back and view that body. I could only imagine the type of therapy that you all would have to seek after that. I knew Dewayne as a client and a friend, but I was nowhere near as close to him as you or anyone else in his family, so I think that puts me in a position to better understand this than you all."

"The doctor that night. What was his name again?" I asked.

"Phillip Bernstein," he let me know, and I mentally stored that name in my head.

"Before I left and went back to Colombia with my family, I was going through the mail, looking at bills, and throwing away the mail that I didn't need. A few things stood out to me that night. First thing that stood out to me is the phone call that was placed from my husband's phone the night of the accident. It was confirmed to us a little bit after midnight that Dewayne didn't survive the accident. If my husband had been dead all that time, then how did he last make a phone call to you at 1:37 A.M on a call that lasted for five minutes and thirty seconds?" I asked, reaching inside my purse and pulling out paperwork of my own.

I showed him the phone logs for that month, and I had it highlighted where Julius could see that he was indeed the last person that Dewayne had talked to that night.

"Oh, and there's more, Julius. Look at these Bank of America statements. Almost fifty thousand dollars was taken from an account ending in 3456 and later transferred into my husbands account. All of which happened after his death. I figured that you were the perfect person to explain some of this to me," I said and again folded my arms and crossed my legs while I waited for him to explain what was going on to me.

"If you look up top at the phone statement, you'll see that these are the statements for Mr. Stewart's work phone. The night of his death, the only cell phone that was found on him was his personal cell. His office phone was left back at the shop, and the reason you see that I was the last call after his death is because Dino, who works at the shop, called me from it since he couldn't reach Mr. Stewart. A simple phone call of almost six minutes took place with me telling Dino what happened and letting him know to tell the other workers about what was going on.

As far as the money you see being moved around in your account, I was informed by Mr. Stewart in his will to distribute all money to his loved ones a week after his death, and that's exactly what I did. The account ending in 3456 is from a savings account. His mother, aunt, Juju, and all other members of the family each have money that was deposited into their accounts from that same account. I didn't want to have to go there with you, but Mrs. Stewart, what exactly is it that your trying to ask me? I'm hearing a lot of beating around the bush as opposed to you just asking me whatever is on your mind. We're adults here, so go ahead and ask," he said.

I released a sigh as I used my hand to push back a few strands of hair behind my ear that were sticking out.

"I want to know if my husband is dead for real," I said, looking him square in his eyes.

"I wish that I could sit here and tell you that he isn't, but he is. I witnessed Mr. Stewart in his last state, which was death. I gain nothing from lying to you, absolutely nothing," he let me know, and I stood up from the chair that I was sitting in.

I slowly walked over and stood behind him. I bent down a little bit, just so that I could whisper in his ear. To any other guy, they probably would have had a hard on by now with me being this close to them, but everyone knew that Julius didn't want anything that I had to offer him. There was no secret that he was gay. It showed in his walk, his talk, and just his all-around appearance. Plus, aside from the business relationship that we all had, we were friends, so he's told us on numerous occasions about his sexuality.

"Julius, if I find out that your telling me anything but the truth, I'm going to make sure that you go down for this. If it's the last thing I do, I will get ALL the right answers. If you are lying, you don't have to worry about me going to the cops because I'll kill you my damn self."

After I said that, I kissed his cheek, and as quickly as I walked into his office, I left just as fast. I wasn't sure if the death certificate was real, and I still wasn't sure if Julius had really even seen Dewayne's body. However, I do know that two of the questions I asked him today was bait, just to see how he would answer, and like the idiot he was, he lied!

There was no phone call placed at 1:37 A.M. I made that entire phone call statement by myself, and he sat his ass there and lied to me about that. On top of that, the money that was deposited into the account didn't come from an account ending in 3456. That was made up too. The last four digits that the money was withdrawn from was 8756. If he could easily lie about that, I couldn't help but wonder what else he was lying to me about?

I wasn't a killer, but I meant what I said to him. If this was just some kind of sick joke that him and Dewayne were in cahoots with, I would make sure to kill him with my bare hands!

CHAPTER FIFTEEN

"Kiondra, come to my office. I need to have a word with you," I said to her on the phone.

Once she assured me that she was on her way, I hung up the office phone and I finished working on the document that was before me. I was at a different Miami office today, and so was Kiondra. This was actually the Miami office that I was going to have Winter working from. She was starting today, and her clock in time was 8:00 A.M. I wanted to see what type of worker she was, which is why it was 7:00 A.M., and I was already in my office.

I was never there at this time of the morning because I paid people to be there at this time to be able to do the hard work for me, but I wanted to see the type of worker Winter was. With this being her first day, and all, I wanted to see if she was the type of worker to get there at exactly 8:00 A.M., or if she was an over achiever and was going to get there earlier than her expected clock in time. I meant what I said to her a week ago about seeing a lot of my ole girl in her. Anyone who knew me or worked for me knew that I took my businesses very serious and that I wasn't just going to hand anybody a job.

I had niggas from around the way who wasn't fuckin' with me because I didn't put them on by handing them a job and letting them work for me. I treated this business like it was my child. You wouldn't just leave your child with anyone to watch them, right? Alright, then that same rule applied when it came to my business. Even friends that I did give jobs to, they had to meet the requirements, do well in an interview, and prove to me that they were more fitting for the job description than someone else.

It may sound a little harsh, but I put blood, sweat, and tears into this shit, so I'll be damned if I hired a motha fucka just because we were cool like that and they came in here working for me and thinking that they could slack off then fuck around and tarnish my whole brand. Even with me seeing Winter and hearing a little bit of her story, at the end of the day, it was still business with me. Meaning, I was giving her thirty days to prove to me that she could do just as good as my last general manager or even better.

I wouldn't fire her if she couldn't meet the expectations, but I would just demote her. Firing her all together would be basically like me taking food out of her and her kids mouth, and I wasn't going to do some fucked up shit like that.

True to my word the night I'd given her the job, I came out the next day and gave her a few more details about the company and her position. I had to have sat with her for over two hours, and as a man, I noticed beauty when I saw it. I bet she didn't even know how beautiful she was. Every time she looked at me and talked, I swear I got lost in those hazel eyes that were damn near golden.

As beautiful as I thought shorty was, I wasn't going to fuck with her like that. I could see it in her eyes and her whole demeanor that all she really cared about right now was getting her shit together, especially for her children, so I was going to allow her to do just that. The best thing I could do for her anyway was put her in a position where she could eat. If I didn't give a fuck, I would have only wanted to take her on a few dates, hit it every chance I got, and kept her in the same position. But because I was a different breed of nigga, I was going to take shorty from her current position, let her boss up, fix her life for her and her kids, and that was worth more than any five star dining or nut from me that she would ever be able to get.

"Hey, I was working on the budget for the new property that you asked me for," Kiondra said, coming inside my office.

Like always, she was in a tight fitting dress, that showed off her nice body. No matter how many times I told shorty to tone down her look, I swear she didn't listen to shit I said. She probably thought that her little dresses and shit would turn a nigga on and have me backtracking and going against my word by fuckin' her again, but once I said I was done with the pussy, I swear I was done, and it was no coming back from it. Because I had other shit to worry about, I didn't even bother to address her look today.

Kiondra's position for the company was basically the secretary. She knew all the ins and outs of each company that I owned, and for the past year, she's been working her ass off to get that general manager position. She knew all the tasks and shit that the general manager needed to do but giving her that position was something that I had to go with my gut instinct on, and I just felt like she wasn't ready for all of that yet.

When she found out that the general manager at this office was leaving, I swear shorty stepped up her game a lot. Every morning, she was bringing a nigga something from Starbucks, she stayed late, came early, but something inside of me just wasn't ready to give her that position yet. There were times in the past when I would need her on big days like company meetings, getting paperwork out to different businesses, and those always happened to be the days that she would call out. I just couldn't fully put my all into her right now. What I did know is that if Winter didn't do a good job in her position, then I was going to hand it to Kiondra.

"Keep the door open, it won't take long," I said.

She nodded as she walked into my office. She didn't bother to sit. Instead, she just stood in front of me and waited for me to let her know what I wanted from her.

"As you know, William is no longer with us…" I started, and a big ass smile crossed her face. and I won't lie, it fucked me up a little bit because I knew where she thought that this conversation was going, but truth is, she and I were on two different pages. "I hired someone to take his spot, and she's supposed to start today. She's supposed to be here at 8:00, and I want you to show her the ropes. Don't teach her no damn short cuts, none of that shit. Train her the same way that you were trained when you started," I let her know.

Hurt and anger flashed across her face.

"Cortez, you're kidding me, right? I work my ass off with this company! There are times when I'm here from sun up to sun down! Every property that you own, no one knows the ins and outs like I do, and you know that! Does that even make sense for you to hire someone new who doesn't even know how to operate this business? You have someone standing in front of you who has the ability to do William's job ten times better than he ever did, yet you just give it to some random person. Why do I feel like your decision is personal? If you and I never had sex, would you have still made this decision?" she asked, and her voice cracked.

"Kiondra, I understand your frustration, but keep in mind that I'm still your boss. The fact that you continue to refer to me as Cortez after I keep telling you to address me as Mr. Anderson is what played into my decision making as well. It makes me question if you even respect me because I shouldn't have to keep telling you to fix something and you continue to do shit your way. Don't even get me started on your work attire. You walk in this bitch every day like you on your way to G5 or Take One as opposed to clocking in at a professional place of business. Increase your listening skills, shorty, and then I'll promote you. Until then, you're going to stay exactly where the fuck you're at.

"If you want to get technical, I'm your boss, therefore I don't owe you an explanation. Like I was saying, I want you to train her today, give her the ropes, and do the shit attitude free. Don't worry about finishing the budget, I'll get someone else to handle that," I let her know.

At the same time, a figure appeared in front of my door. I looked at the time on my Apple watch and saw that it was 7:30 A.M. It was Winter standing on the other side of the door. *Shit, she was beautiful.* She was nowhere near dressed like how Kiondra was dressed, but she still had the ability to stand out. She wore a pair of black slacks with a long sleeved silk dress shirt and a pair of low heels on her feet.

Shorty didn't have any type of make-up on her face, but I could see the perfection of her face all the way from here. I fucked with the short cut that she wore that was similar to the way Keri Hilson used to rock her shit. She had a purse on her shoulder and a lunch box in her hands, looking like a rookie in true form on her first day of work. Only woman I ever looked at like this in my life was Amari, so this was strange as fuck to me.

"Oh, ummm, I'm sorry. The receptionist told me to head to the back. I'll wait outside until the two of you finish talking," she called out, and I stood up from the chair that I was sitting in.

"It's cool, come inside," I called, and she did just that.

"Winter, this is Kiondra, the secretary. Kiondra, this is Winter, the new general manager that I was telling you about," I said, introducing the two of them.

"Hi, nice to meet you, Kiondra," Winter said and held her hand out for Kiondra to shake, but she left her hanging.

"What college did you graduate from?" Kiondra asked.

I didn't interrupt because I wanted to see how far she could go, so she could give me a reason to suspend her ass for at least a week.

"I didn't attend college," Winter let her know, and Kiondra released a sarcastic laugh followed by shaking her head.

"Oh, okay, so you got the job based on your looks and your hazel eyes then, right? Cortez, this isn't fair, and you know it," Kiondra let me know.

"Yo, I just told you a minute ago that I don't have to explain shit to you on why I make the decisions that I make. If you feeling some type of way about my decision, it's plenty of ways you can get out of this motha fucka. We got stairs, elevators, and if you feeling brave, you can even jump your ass out the window if you want to. One monkey won't stop no show sweetheart, so always remember that. Like I was saying, this is Winter, the new general manager, and I want you to show her the ropes. Let me know if you can't do it because I'll stop what I'm doing and do it myself, and you can go home," I let her know, sounding like the head nigga in charge that I was.

"I can do it," she finally said right before she walked out of the office, leaving it just Winter and I in the office.

"I apologize about you having to see that, especially on your first day. If you feel like she's not training you the way that she should be or that she has an attitude or some shit, let me know. Don't keep that shit in because your job depends on it, shorty. Like I told you back at the shelter, I'm putting you on a thirty-day probation, so you only have thirty days to show and prove. Go ahead to the back. It's going to be the last door on the right. I'll tell Kiondra to meet you there."

"Okay. Thank you again," she said before she turned on her heels and walked out of the office.

A FEW HOURS later

"Knock! Knock! Knock!"

"Come in," I called out after I stood up and turned my desktop off.

It was a little after 1:00 P.M., and I was about to head out because I had a meeting at 2:00 at another office. I looked up and noticed that it was my receptionist, Brenda.

Brenda just worked here part time because she was a full-time college student, so this was just a little something for her to do on the side. She was a young girl, in her twenties or something like that. Her uncle worked for the company, and it was him who'd put a good word in for her, so that's how she was able to come and get an interview with me where she was hired on the spot. It really wasn't much that her job entitled. She was simply the person who answered the phones, sent out emails, let me know when someone was there to visit me, and little shit like that.

For the job she had, all I really was looking for was a high school diploma. She had about another year left in college, where she was pursuing a degree in accounting. I told her a while back to make sure she showed me her degree when she graduated because I had a nice little position for her. That's just the type of nigga I was; a solid one, making sure that if those around me were dedicated and I was in a position to help them, then I was going to do that shit.

"I know you were getting ready to leave, but I wanted to let you know that I called a few of the restaurants that were on the list, and majority of the ones that you requested aren't able to accommodate a party of fifty tonight. Barton G has given us the option of renting it out for the night. Is that what you want to do?" she asked, and I sucked my teeth after realizing that it was indeed the third Monday of the month.

Every third Monday of the month, I took my top workers out to dinner as basically my way of saying thank you. We would get together and talk about expanding the business.

"That's fine. Make sure you send out an email, so everyone knows where we're meeting," I let her know, and she assured me that she had it right before she walked out of my office.

Lord knows I didn't feel like being around a bunch of people tonight. All I was thinking about doing when I made it home was rolling up a fat blunt, kicking my feet up, and chilling with my bitches (dogs). I was on some chill shit tonight, not even wanting any pussy, but I knew that everyone looked forward to these Mondays, so I wasn't going to cancel it. My weed and my dogs would still be there when I made it home.

I finally finished up in my office, and on my way out the door, I had to pass by the break room. I could see her from the side as she sat down at the table eating her lunch. I laughed to myself because shorty came prepared with her lunch box and everything. She was the only one inside because majority of the people who worked here would normally go out for lunch. It was her first day and shorty didn't have any friends, which was why she was eating by herself. Although I should have been on my way out the door because where I was going wasn't just around the corner, I managed to open the door anyway.

As soon as I walked in, her eyes fell on mine, and it didn't take a rocket scientist to know that her first day was hell so far. I could see the shit all in her eyes.

"How's your training going?" I asked, taking the chair that was right next to hers.

"It's a lot of information to take in, but I'll be fine. I'm thinking about my kids. I told them that we should be able to have our own place soon, and they are pretty much counting down the days," she let me know, and I nodded.

"Before you know it, you'll be able to do all of this shit that she in there training you for with your eyes closed. Years ago, I went into this business thinking it was going to be easy money and an easy job, but I was wrong. Shit ain't easy running a business, and it damn sure isn't any easier to find people that you can trust who will try to run the business as good as I do. A lot of shit goes into keeping this shit together, but hard work and dedication are what keeps these walls up. Shit is always going to be hard your first time doing something, but that's why you practice. The more you practice this shit, the easier it's going to get. You'll be alright shorty," I said then stood up from the chair that I was sitting in and pushed it back in.

"I'm not sure what you had planned tonight, but the third Monday of every month, we all get together to have dinner. If you not busy, you can come on by. This is basically the part where I thank everybody with dinner for the part that they play in the company," I let her know right before I opened the door to leave.

"I won't make any promises, but I'll try to be there," she let me know, and that was that.

CHAPTER SIXTEEN

My feet were killing me. Here I was, sitting in the last row of the bus after a long first day of work, and my feet were crying in my heels. I've never really been a heels type of girl. I was always into sandals and sneakers. I knew that I couldn't go into the job on my first day with either of those on, which was why I had to wear heels. The thing about it was that the heels on my feet weren't even high. If anything, they were just snug and uncomfortable as hell.

My whole outfit came from the mini-mall in the shelter. I picked out a week's worth of clothes. I didn't have to come out of my pocket for any of the things, and all of the outfits that I had chosen had price tags still on them, meaning that these clothes were brand new. I was so thankful that the shelter had provided us with clothes because the way I was pinching my money together, I couldn't afford to go anywhere and get a whole new wardrobe.

Aside from the pain in my feet, today was alright. Considering the opportunity that Cortez had given me, I didn't want to complain, but boy did I wish someone else could be the one to train me. I wouldn't say that I didn't like Kiondra because I didn't know her well enough not to like her, but I will say that she had a nasty attitude. Everything she showed me today, she showed it to me in a way that made me feel like I was a burden to her, or as if I was even slow.

I was pretty sure she thought that being rude to me was going to make me give up, but if only she knew who raised me. Compared to Sandra, she was America's sweetheart. It didn't take a rocket scientist to notice that she either had a major crush on Cortez or the two of them had had relations in the past. I knew that it was so much deeper than me getting the position over her. I had no idea why the hell she was so uptight or even jealous because there was literally nothing going on between Cortez and me. I thought he was a nice person, and I was very appreciative of him giving me the job, and that's as far as anything that he and I had going on went.

Of course, I thought he was sexy, but what woman didn't? What made him even more attractive than he already was, was the fact that he was a boss! God, that turned me on. When he snapped on Kiondra today back in his office in front of me, I swear I got a tingly feeling in my pussy just from watching him take control and check her. It was the way he swaggered around in those expensive ass suits, as if he didn't have a care in the damn world. I had love for a boss, but since he was my boss, I probably would never admit that to him. It would be very unprofessional of me, and I wasn't trying to do anything that would hinder my position at the company.

The bus had finally come to my stop, and I got off. With me starting a new job that had new hours, Anita would keep the kids for me during the day, which she told me a hundred times that she didn't mind at all. I promised her that when I received my first paycheck that I was going to pay her, but she insisted on telling me that I didn't owe her a damn thing.

On the bus ride home, I was thinking about the dinner that Cortez had invited me to. After the long day that I'd just had, I could use it because I can't remember the last time that I had a night out to have dinner and enjoy myself. Not that I'm complaining or anything, but my life revolved around my children, so I never really got a chance to kick back and have a night to myself. It had been this way for years, even when Dewayne was in the picture. He barely did anything with me and the children because he always made it seem like he was so tired from work, when really, the only thing that his ass was tired of was all of that damn lying he was doing.

On the opposing side, I didn't want Anita to feel like I was dropping the kids off with her too much. On the walk to Anita's house, I thought about what I was going to do. Before I knew it, I was standing on her porch, knocking on her front door, and I hadn't even made up my mind yet.

"Mommyyyyy!" I heard both of my children yelling from inside the house.

I swear my heart melted at the sound of their little voices. I could hear the lock turning, and I knew it was Anita opening the door for them. Once it was open, they both bombarded me with hugs and kisses. Nothing could ever compare to this moment as I kneeled and accepted their kisses while doing the same thing to them in return.

"Auntie Anita is going to bake a chocolate cake, Mommy. Can we stay for some? Pleaseee?" my beautiful daughter asked me.

This little girl loved her some chocolate, so much so that she and her brother had been stealing it from Sandra's dresser when we were staying with her. Both my kids were the total opposite of me when it came to candy eating because I rarely ate candy, and I couldn't stand chocolate.

"She heard me on the phone saying that I was going to bake a cake. Ever since then, she's been telling me to ask you if they could stay the night for some," Anita said right before she leaned in and gave me a hug.

Although Anita looked nowhere near how she used to look when I was younger, she was still that mother figure that I had always yearned for. As a little girl, it was she who would buy my sister and I Christmas gifts, gifts for our birthdays, or just because gifts, making it feel like she was our mother instead of Sandra. Although Sandra was the one who birthed me, I used to wish that it was Anita when I was a little girl since she was so loving and caring.

"My boss invited me out to dinner tonight. It's something that they all do the third Monday of the month, and I was thinking about going. It starts at eight. I can come and get them when I'm done," I said to Anita, and she smiled.

"Please go. You deserve to do something besides go to work, Winter. I have been telling you for months now that I will watch the kids while you have a day off to just pamper yourself. That fifty dollars that you give me, which I keep telling you that I don't need, so when you're not looking, I slide it right back in your purse. I keep telling you to use that on you. Go and get your nails done or some shit. Get these thick ass eyebrows arched. You do a good job on your own hair, so you don't have to really worry about that department. Winter, it's okay to think about you for a change. I watch the way you are with these kids, and you done got so wrapped up in this that you've forgotten just who the hell Winter is and what Winter deserves. Enjoy your night out. I got the babies," she assured me.

I thought about what she said, and I smiled while I nodded my head because she was right.

"I want to meet this boss of yours that you've been talking about since the day he gave you that good old job," Anita said as she and I took a seat on the living room couch. "He's sexy, isn't he?" she asked me, making me laugh.

"Anita, sexy isn't the word. Then, he has the nerve to walk around in these suits that just fit his body so damn perfectly. That beard, those tattoos that I saw on him, his dimples, those waves, just everything about that man is sexy. All I can do is lust over him, though, because it won't go anywhere. The woman that was training me today, I believe that they had something going on before or she likes him. She's the type of woman that I see him with. I just feel like he likes those type, with the slim-thick body, the big booty, and all of that stuff that I for sure don't have. I got two kids, Anita. I'm still holding on to baby fat from three years ago, so I'm way off his radar," I told her, and she looked at me like I was crazy, right before she shook her head.

"Who the hell even put that negative shit in your head? Dewayne or was it Sandra? It had to be Sandra's ass. You're a fool for even believing some nonsense like that about yourself. I remember when you were a little girl, I always used to say that if I had a daughter, I wish she would look just like you. Winter, you are gorgeous. I see nothing wrong with your body either. I see a thick woman who has some meet on her bones, and if any man sees otherwise, then he's probably gay. I'm not just saying this because of the relationship that I have with you either. I'm saying it because it's the truth. Never feel like a man is too good for you. You are a woman, you are the catch, so you should have the confidence of feeling like you are too good for any man. Don't you ever forget that either," she let me know.

Anita and I talked for a few minutes more before I stood and let her know that I would be back for my kids later tonight. My own damn children had dismissed me for some damn chocolate cake. Seeing how happy they were tonight about getting some of Anita's chocolate cake made me that much more excited about getting our own place. I couldn't wait for those nights that I would come home from a long day of work and I cook them their favorite meals. I swear that that was something worth looking forward to.

After another bus ride and some walking, I was finally back at the shelter. On the ridet here, I thought about the few clothes that I had and which outfit I would wear tonight. I knew that I had a pair of jeans with a nice top that I could pair it with and some sandals. It wasn't the prettiest outfit, but it was going to work for tonight.

I'll admit that a big part of me was only going to this dinner tonight so that I could be around Cortez. Hell, I was such a closed in, timid person, that I didn't even care to be around a lot of people, so I was only going so I could see him. I was hoping that Kiondra didn't show up tonight. I had dealt with too much of her today, so I wanted to be free of her tonight since she would have to train me again in the morning.

Walking inside, I spotted my bunk mate, Teagan. She had her daughter sitting on her bed, and Teagan's back was turned to me as she hurriedly threw clothes together in a duffle bag.

"Hey, T. You going somewhere?" I asked.

She jumped when she heard my voice then turned around and looked at me. For whatever reason, I could sense nervousness all in her body language.

"Oh, hey, Winter. Ummm, no. I'm not going anywhere… I just… I have… I have to do some laundry. Where are the babies?" she asked, referring to my twins since she didn't see them with me.

"Anita is going to babysit them for me tonight while I go to dinner. Is everything alright with you?" I asked then took a seat on my bed and finally removing my shoes.

"Yeah, girl, I'm fine. Just a long day, that's all. Look, I'm about to go and do this laundry. If I don't see you after you finish getting ready and everything, I hope you have a good night. I'm happy to see you getting out," she said right before she walked up on me and hugged me tight.

I mean, her hug was super tight. She was hugging me similar to the way that I hugged my children. Not only was her hug tight, but it was long as well. Maybe it was just one of those days for her that she could use a hug. Once she hugged me, her daughter Meagan came over and hugged me next, and just like that, the two of them were in the direction of the laundry room.

7:57 P.M.

I was running super late to the dinner, which was set to start in another three minutes. I'd been standing at the bus stop for the past twenty minutes or so, and a bus had yet to come. I ended up having to download the Uber app and make an account really fast. After putting my card on file, a few minutes later, I'd requested myself a ride. I'd never done this before, although I've heard a lot about it. Thankfully, I now had my own phone that I paid the bill for and a new bank about. It was either this, or stand around and wait for the bus, that was going to have me later than what I already was.

I had to dig into the little savings account that I had for this ride since it was taking me down to Miami Beach and the ride was pretty pricey. In another five minutes or so, the Chevy Cruze car finally pulled up in the plaza that I was now waiting in, and I jumped in the backseat. The whole time I was back there, my palms were sweaty.

My driver was a white guy who looked to be in his mid-thirties. I kept the phone dialed to 911 just in case he did anything funny and I had to click send and make the phone call. I probably was doing a bit too much, but it was for my sanity. He was nice, though. He offered me the aux cord, so I could play my music, but I declined. He had a little plastic bowl up front with all types of sweets in it, which he offered me as well, but I declined again. If Sandra had taught me anything, it was not to take shit from strangers that I didn't see them purchase themselves. After I declined his offers, he drove with the radio at a minimum volume and nothing else was said between the two of us, which was fine with me because I could use some time with my thoughts.

It took us about thirty more minutes to pull up to the restaurant, which had me getting out of the car at 8:45, making me forty- five minutes late. I hoped that this wasn't one of those things that I had to be on time for, especially with me being on probation with the company and everything.

"Hello. Welcome to Barton G. Will you be joining the

party for tonight?" the pretty, female hostess asked me the moment I walked into the restaurant.

"Hello. Yes, I am," I let her know.

"Right this way," she said, and I followed her.

The more we walked, the more I realized that Boss wasn't just something that they called him for the hell of it. They called him Boss because that's truly what he was. This man had rented out the entire restaurant. I had noticed that when I didn't see any other parties there. This man was way out of my league, and I was okay with that.

We finally walked into a room which held two long tables, and it looked as if each table could seat at least twenty people. I felt my hands begin to sweat when it felt like everyone in the room was looking at me. God, I wanted to just crawl up in a hole and die. No one had told me that the attire for tonight was damn near formal. Almost all the men in attendance were in nice suits or just a nice dress shirt and some slacks. Then, there was the women who had me feeling very insecure about myself. I mean, these women's faces were beat as if they were about to do a photoshoot for makeup. There were fancy Chanel, Louis Vuitton, and Berkin bags resting on the back of these women's chairs. They were dressed in Christian Louboutin heels, Steve Madden, and the clothes they wore had to be clothes from designer stores out of Bal Harbour shops.

For a second, I was mad at Cortez because he didn't say anything about dressing up like I was going to the Grammy's. Then again, Barton G was an upscale restaurant, so I guess the name should have been all the confirmation that I needed to dress up. I thought that I was doing something when I left out tonight in my skinny jeans, dressy shirt, and the blazer that I'd paired it with. Instead of the sandals that I was previously going to wear, I ended up putting back on the same heels that I was just complaining about hurting my feet. All eyes were on me. I was pretty sure that everyone who didn't know me was trying to figure out just were the hell I fit into all of this, and sadly, I was trying to figure that out too.

"Winter. Come on. We just put our order in like ten minutes ago. You're not that late," his deep voice boomed out. "Zachery, take that empty seat and let Winter sit right here," Cortez said to one of the men who was sitting next to him named Zachery.

He quickly got up, and once I was near the chair, he pushed the chair back a little bit so that I could have room to get in, and then he pushed me up more to the table. I smiled at his gentlemanly ways because these days, it was as if chivalry didn't exist anymore. I quickly thanked him, and he assured me that it wasn't a big deal before he walked off and he took the other empty seat.

"Everyone, let me get your attention," Cortez said as he sat at the head of the table.

God, he looked so good tonight in that olive green suit. He smelled so damn good too. I wanted to divert my attention away from him because I didn't know if it was obvious that I was sitting there lusting over him, but he was getting ready to start talking, so I had no choice but to look at him. You'd be a fool not to look at him when he talked, especially since his presence alone already demanded so much attention. I'd just seen him today and, in a few hours,, it looked as if he'd got more good looking. He sat at the head of the table, but he stood to make his announcement.

"Everybody, this is Winter. Winter is the new general manager at the Miami office. She started today. Ya'll be nice to her and show her some love," Cortez said, and the table erupted in applause.

Granted, everyone was looking at me, especially with me just now being introduced and all, but I could literally feel heat from across the room. That's when I looked over and I saw that it was Kiondra. She'd come out tonight, and if looks could kill, I would be dead. She was sitting amongst a group of women who were all dressed nicely. Maybe this time it was because Cortez had announced in front of everyone that he wanted me to sit next to him. Who knows?

In my defense, I felt that the only reason he'd offered me to sit next to him was that technically he was the only one in the room who I somewhat knew. I was glad he'd done that because everyone else already had their little cliques, but if it was going to have people hating me, then I didn't care for the attention.

"Mr. Anderson, aren't you going to tell Winter the dinner rule? You know, whoever is the last person to get here has to be the one to leave the tip," Kiondra said from her side of the table.

This woman really couldn't stand me, and I didn't see why. I looked at Cortez and watched as his jaws clenched, and then he took a sip of whatever was inside his glass.

"It's her first dinner, so I'll let her get a pass. Not everybody goes home at the end of the workday and all they have to do is get ready for dinner. Other people have different priorities, such as children. When have I ever been an asshole when it came to anyone and their situation with their children? Mind your business for a second, Kiondra, and be nice to Winter because you never know, she may be the one to sign your checks," Cortez said.

There was a bunch of ooooh's from the table with some added laughter. I could tell that she was pissing him off from the three lines that had appeared on his forehead. This was the second time today that she had gotten him this upset.

"If you don't put her in her place, she's going to keep trying you. The moment you put your foot down, I bet you won't have any more problems out of her ass," Cortez leaned in to tell me.

It was as if everyone was looking at us. It was obvious that they were trying to figure out what he was telling me, but it was only loud enough for me to hear him. I nodded, letting him know that I got it.

A few minutes later, the waitress came over and just took my order since I was the only one who hadn't ordered. While I was ordering, the table was having a conversation about different types of rent promotions that were going on for the next month. Basically, something to attract more tenants mixed with something that the company has never done before. I listened to everything that everyone was saying and took everything in. They were specifically talking about the condos that Cortez owned in Fort Lauderdale; the ones where the minimum rent was $3,500. I knew that because I saw the charts earlier today with Kiondra.

"I don't see the purpose of having a promotion. If someone is willing to pay $3,500, then let them because it's obvious that they have it. When you're the best, why give people promotions that they have no problem paying for? Do you ever see companies like Gucci, Louis Vuitton, or those other high-end stores having promotion deals? No, you don't because the name alone is going to sell itself." Kiondra asked that silly question and made such a silly statement.

Had she worded what she had said a little differently, I would have agreed with her to a certain extent, but she said it in a way that indicated that the customer was the least of her worries and she didn't care about somehow giving back. In my opinion, that was the only way that the company was going to grow. Yes, the statement that she made in terms to Gucci and those other stores was true, but it wasn't in the company's policy to be anything like those stores. I'd been quiet the whole night, but I figured that this was the time where I jumped in. Plus, I wanted to impress Cortez, so I sat up in my chair and cleared my throat.

"If ever you or anyone in the company feel that way, then you've become cocky, which isn't a good thing. If it weren't for the residents living in these units, then we would all be without a job because revenue wouldn't be coming into the company; revenue and clientele. So, is it really smart to try to get one over on the residents or to have a cocky attitude toward them? It's almost summer, meaning that June is coming up. Everyone knows that June is pretty much the busiest month in terms of moving in or moving out.

"For example, the condos Blue Aqua in Fort Lauderdale that we're talking about is in major competition with Farm Red that's across the street. I don't know about you, but after doing a little research on Farm Red today at the office, they have a promotion going on for one hundred dollars off the first month's rent. That's called a promotion. That's called people ringing the phone lines inquiring about getting on the waiting list. We don't have to have to take off one hundred dollars for the first months rent. We can do something like waive the application fee or taking fifty dollars off the security deposit, anything to show that we are a company that looks at the needs of our residents.

"To simply say that we don't have to do promotions because they can afford it is kind of ignorant. Look at Publix with the buy one get one free. Walmart and its low prices. The people can afford it, yet these two major competitors always has some type of promotion going on," I said, ending her whole theory.

My recommendations had gotten all types of applause, and the only thing left for Kiondra to do was pick up her jaw from the floor. When it came to having debates, that's pretty much always been my strong point, so it was no big deal to me that I'd easily crushed Kiondra.

"You might have done something with that one," one of

the men said to Cortez, referring to me as he reached his hand out and the two of them pounded each other up.

I smiled when I saw Cortez smiling because I could tell that I made him happy tonight. I don't know what had come over me, but for the duration of dinner, I found myself engaging in conversation with the table, speaking up, introducing new thoughts and ideas that I felt would be good for the company, and I can honestly say that when it was time to wrap everything up, I found myself not wanting to leave.

I went from walking into this room a couple of hours ago and feeling like I didn't fit in to fitting in perfectly. Oh, I forgot to even talk about the steak and the mashed potatoes that I'd eaten. This was easily the best steak that I'd ever tasted in my life. Dinner was over, and everyone was outside either standing around or walking to their cars. I, on the other hand, was standing with my phone in my hand requesting another Uber. It was almost midnight, and I didn't know where to walk to for a bus, so I felt like getting another Uber was my best bet.

"How you getting home?" his deep voice cooed from behind me.

Even if I didn't recognize his voice, I would have still known it was him from the smell of his cologne. I turned around, only to see that he was standing directly behind me. If he were to have gotten any closer, I swear I would have been able to feel his dick on my backside.

"Uber. That's how I got out here," I let him know.

He pulled down on his beard before he scanned the area,

almost as if he was looking to see if anyone was paying us any attention.

"I got you. You don't need to be getting in a car with no fuckin' stranger anyway. It's some crazy motha fuckas in this world, shorty," he said. His voice was so hard and aggressive, but damn was it coming off in a protective way, if that made any sense.

"It's not just one stop I have to make. I have to get my kids and then go back to the… well, you know," I said, not really wanting to say it. I knew he wouldn't judge me, but still.

"Like I said, I got you. Let me tell everyone good night, and then we can head out," Cortez told me.

It took him about five minutes to head over to where a lot of the people were standing, and then he finally walked back over to me. For whatever reason, I was nervous walking next to him. I guess because of the awkward silence; it made me feel a little anxious. The only sounds coming from outside were of the voices that we could hear lingering in the background, mixed with the beautiful sounds of the Miami breeze.

I'm not sure why I was so shocked when he pulled his keys out, and all of a sudden, he started the car without us being inside. He was driving a matte black, 2019 Mercedes G wagon. I could have died because this car was so beautiful. I don't know why, but I was expecting him to be driving some sort of sports car or something. This was nice, though, and it fit him.

Anita used to always tell me that a man's car said a lot

about the kind of person he was, and she was right. This car screamed power, dominance, boss, and sexy, all of which were synonyms of Cortez. Like the perfect gentleman, when we neared the car, he walked over to the passenger side and opened the door for me.

My body literally sank into the custom red seats, and as soon as I put my seat belt on, he went ahead and closed the door. The car had a smell of weed mixed with that new car smell. In a few more seconds, he joined me inside the car, and instantly, the car paired with his phone from the Bluetooth. To my surprise, Sir Charles' "Is There Anybody Lonely?" began to play.

I smiled to myself because I just knew that some rap music was going to come on where the men would call women everything but a child of God. The sexiest thing happened in the car when he started nodding his head to the beat of the music, and in such a mannish way, he raised his hand to snap to the beat as well. Just the little things that he was doing tonight was causing a flood in my panties, so there was no doubt in my mind that I would have to take another shower once I made it back to the shelter.

"Tell me a little bit about yourself, Winter. What's your story?" he asked now that he was jumping on the highway, after I'd keyed in the address to Anita's house on the navigation system.

"Ummm, it's not really much to tell about me. I grew up right here in Miami. My mom raised me and my older sister, Summer. I met a guy while I was working at Walmart, and he later became my boyfriend. I had the twins by him, we were engaged shortly after that, and he passed away a few months ago. I'm not sure if that's what you intended for me to tell when you asked me to tell you my story, but I was serious when I said that there really isn't much to tell," I told him.

In the midst of him driving, he kept looking over at me. I should have been terrified by him not keeping his eyes on the road, but for whatever reason, I was comfortable. It was like I knew that no harm would happen while I was in his presence.

"I'm sorry for your loss, shorty. As kids, we need our fathers in our lives. That shit is important as hell. I'm talking about the fathers who actually do for their children, though," he said, and I heard a little bit of hostility in his voice when he said that, making me believe he had some type of bad history with his father, but I wasn't going to ask.

"No need to apologize to me. When he died, the truth was revealed. Come to find out, this man had a whole wife, and they had children of their own. I was basically just his side piece. I let that go on right up under my nose for four years, and had he still been alive, I'm pretty sure that it would have still been happening. It's a situation that I don't really like to talk about because I don't need anyone judging me on my naïveté," I told him.

"You said that your ole girl raised you. Where is she?" he asked, quickly switching the subject.

I wondered if he switched it because out of respect for me, he didn't want to talk bad Dewayne, or if it had anything to do with me saying that this was a topic that I didn't care to talk too much about.

"She's alive. She literally stays a few blocks from the shelter," I let him know.

I was talking to him and looking at him, so I could see the way his jaws flexed a little bit. There was that sense of protectiveness again. A sense of me feeling like he actually cared.

"And she knows about your living arrangements right now?" he asked. I nodded that she did. "That's your family, so I won't speak too much on that shit, but that's foul, yo'. No amount of anger in my heart will ever allow me to willingly let my child and my grandchild stay at a shelter. Granted, the shelter is owned by my ol' girl, and I know that she's going to do whatever in her power to make sure that ya'll straight, but it's the principle.

"From the sound of things, your ole girl is heartless. That's how my ole boy was with us growing up. He used to beat the shit out of me, my ole girl, and my oldest sister. I hated that man since I was about two years old. It wasn't until I was fifteen that we all finally got the fuck away from that shit. On some real shit, I was hoping that his black ass was dead, but a couple of months ago, I ran into him. And you want to know where that bastard is staying?" he asked, again taking his focus from off the road and looking down at me.

"Where?" I inquired.

"Living in an apartment with his girlfriend at one of my properties in a wheelchair with only one leg left. I can't even begin to tell you the rage that I felt when I saw his ass. Thoughts in my head were telling me to pull his ass out that wheelchair and beat on him the same way he used to beat on us, but I felt like I would be a coward if he did that, especially with him not being able to fully defend himself. That's the difference between him and I though.

"We weren't able to defend ourselves back then, yet he would still beat our asses. You know I didn't even tell my ole girl or my sisters that I ran into him? My ole girl put up with a lot of shit from him over the years, and she's happy in the space that she's in right now, so I don't want to bring him up and have her back tracking. Fuck him!" he spat.

I just wanted to reach over the seat and hug him because I could hear it in his voice that not only was he angry with his dad, but he was also upset. Those deep, dark stories of our past had quieted down the conversation in the car, so for the duration of the ride, we were both left with our thoughts. In about another fifteen minutes, we pulled up to Anita's house. I was removing myself from the seatbelt when Cortez all of a sudden gently grabbed my arm, stopping me from getting out.

"I can easily change your living arrangements around for you, Winter, if you want me to. I have two, three, and even four-bedroom condos that I can have you in first thing tomorrow morning. Although that's my ole girl's building and what not, I know how bad you want to get you and your kids up out of that shit, although you don't really say it. Let me help you out, shorty," his deep voice boomed to me.

God, I was so turned on. It was the way his eyes were fixed on me as he talked. That four-bedroom condo sounded so tempting, but I just couldn't, so I shook my head.

"Cortez, you have already done more than enough. You put me in a position to put my kids and I in something nice in a couple of weeks or so. Not to compare you to my ex fiancé or anything like that, but the last time I put my all into a guy and let a guy do nice gestures for me, it left me and my kids high and dry. Anything that I get, whether it be for me or my kids, I want to be the one to do it because I never want to give anyone the satisfaction of ever taking shit away from me again. You can respect that, right?" I asked, and he released a sigh.

"I respect it. Hell, I respect the fuck out of you because of the type of person that you are. I'm not the type of nigga that will give something to somebody though and take it back. I don't move like that, but I get that you want to be able to make shit happen on your own. I got it," he said, throwing his hands up in surrender, basically letting me know that he was going to go with the flow.

I was getting my point across to him, so it had caused me to lean in a little bit closer. Then, when he was the one to get his point across, it caused him to lean in as well, so technically, we were pretty close. On the drive over, he'd placed a piece of Winterfresh gum in his mouth, so I could literally smell it on his breath.

He was looking at me, and I was looking at him. It was like we were daring each other with our own eyes to lean in for a kiss. I'd been lusting over this man pretty much all day, and I didn't know the next time that I was going to ever be this close to him, so I put on my big girl panties then leaned in and kissed him. I'm not sure why, but I was somewhat prepared for him to curve me and to let me know that I was being unprofessional, but that moment never came. In fact, his big, strong hands went to the back of my neck, and he passionately kissed me back. My right hand rested on his chest while the other one was in my lap, and I hungrily kissed him.

I'd never been this horny in my life. In fact, it was a painful feeling because my clit was thumping so much, which was causing me discomfort. Cortez was a great kisser. I hated tongue kissing with Dewayne because it would always be so rushed, and he was a messy kisser, but this kiss right here could be voted number one kiss in the rule book. I could feel my body getting hot, and that's when he pulled away from me.

"Shit! Go and get your kids, shorty. Ima wait out here," Cortez said, and I didn't have to look in a mirror to know that my face was flushed red from embarrassment.

I don't know if he regretted the kiss, but I didn't. I was too afraid to look at him, so I quickly got out of th
and walked up to Anita's door
times. She came to the door witl
was sleeping, and my son right
nosey, so she was looking past my
the car parked outside, it's like s
Cortez, so she smiled. She said n

was sure she was already forming her own opinion in her head.

"Thank you, Anita," I said after she passed Storm to me.

"Anytime, Winter. You know that," she said.

With Storm sleeping on me and as I held onto my son's hand, we walked to the car. Cortez was now out of the car. He came around and helped me put the twins in the back. My son was usually so inquisitive that he would always ask me a million questions, but he didn't even question me on Cortez. He just simply fell back asleep along with his sister.

On the ride to the shelter, there was nothing said between Cortez and me. I was counting down the seconds to get back to the shelter because I was so embarrassed. The moment he pulled the car into an empty spot, I quickly got out and headed to the back to get Storm. I grabbed Junior and stood him by my side.

"Thank you again for the ride," I said to Cortez, and then I tried to walk away.

"Why you acting like that, Winter? Just know I pulled away because I respect you. If I had pulled you in my seat and proceeded to blow your back out, just know that I wouldn't have had any respect for you. Remember that," he said then leaned in and kissed my forehead.

Did this man just give me a forehead kiss? Every woman knew what the forehead kiss exemplified. I didn't bother [illegible]onding, though, I just simply walked away, but the [illegible] smile was on my face. As soon as we made it inside, [illegible] quietly with my kids so that I couldn't wake [illegible] quickly laid them down on their bed. When I set my things on top of my bed, I saw a letter with my name on it.

Kicking my heels off, I opened the letter and saw that it had come from Teagan. It's crazy because I was just questioning in my head where the hell she and Meagan had gone because, when I came in, I didn't see them in their beds.

Dear Winter,

I hate that I have to leave on short notice, but earlier today, while I was in Target, I ran into Malcom. He didn't do any of the things that I expected him to do when he saw me. In fact, he cried when he saw me and Meagan. He promised me that he'd changed, and I believe him this time, Winter. I know that the physical abuse will no longer happen. I'm giving him one more chance because although he put me through a lot, I still love him.

I know we talked about moving in together with our children, but you honestly don't need me. You just received that big money paying job, so enjoy your life and take care of those beautiful kids. Kiss them for me too. I'm grateful to have met a friend like you, Winter. I love you.

A tear fell from my eyes when I finished reading the letter because I knew that her going back to her ex wasn't going to end well. I cried because of the stories that she'd told me about the two of them, and I knew he was going to harm her again. I could feel it.

CHAPTER SEVENTEEN

It's been one month since I had the suspicions about my husband cheating on me during his trip to LA. Either I'd lost my sixth sense, or I was just flat out wrong about Neo cheating. I had yet for a bitch to come to me as a woman, so I could have been wrong all along. I wouldn't say that we were back to how we used to be, but I wasn't angry with him anymore, especially now that it was looking like I was wrong after all.

So, it's Thursday night, and my husband called me earlier to let me know that he wanted shrimp alfredo for dinner. Like the good wife, here I was, dressed in my apron, making my husband's favorite. The fact that Neo was even eating my cooking again had proved to me that in his heart, he really thought that I wasn't upset with him anymore. If he didn't, he wouldn't eat shit that I made. Let's just say that there have been times in the past that I've put laxatives in the things that I've cooked for him due to him fuckin' up. I was trying to change, so I wasn't going to even play around like that with him tonight.

He'd just come in the house a few minutes ago from work, and right now, he was in the shower. My husband's showers lasted just as long as mine, so he would probably be up there for a few minutes more. The alfredo was done, and I'd just taken the bread from out of the oven. I went ahead and fixed both of our plates and left a glass of wine on the table. My stomach was rumbling, and I was trying to wait for him, so we could eat together, but he was taking forever in the bathroom.

I ended up jogging up the steps, only to get into our bedroom and see that he still had the shower running, which only meant that he wasn't even done.

"Baby, hurry up. I'm starving," I said, walking into the bathroom.

His dreads were hanging down his back as he showered, and his dick was hanging too. God, I wanted to jump in there with him, but the food that I'd just finished cooking was calling my name.

"You know I like to shit before I get in the shower. Give me two more minutes, baby. Don't eat without me," he called out.

I walked out of the bathroom, making sure to close the door behind me. As soon as I was getting ready to walk out of the bedroom, I heard his phone chime. Now, any other time, I didn't pay his cell phone any attention, but because I'd been having my suspicions lately, I ended up checking it out. Yes, in the past, I felt like I had to go through Neo's phone and shit, but I can honestly say that I have outgrown that stage.

I felt like the dumb ass twenty-year-old girl that I was from years ago as I keyed in the password to his phone, which was my birthday. The first thing that I saw on the screen had me placing my hand over my chest. When he'd locked his phone, he'd forgotten to close out of the Cashapp app, so I saw where he'd just sent $10,000 dollars to *Tiana305.*

I just knew that this wasn't the same Tiana from the past. A bitch who was fuckin' on my man every time I turned my back. Hell no, Neo couldn't have been that fuckin' stupid. That was the same bitch who had caused him to come so close to losing me in the first place. Even if it wasn't her, what the fuck was he doing sending a bitch that much money? I was so wrapped up in the Cashapp, that I'd totally forgotten why I'd chosen to touch his phone in the first place.

I dragged the notifications down from the top of the screen, and that's when I saw he had a text message from an LA area code. The message was thanking him for the money for Neona. Who the fuck was Neona? The only Neona that I knew was my daughter who I lost almost two months ago. There were numerous text messages between my husband and this person, and each time, he would address the person as Tiana, so this had to be that bitch. Did this nigga have a daughter? That's what it was looking like.

My hands were shaking so badly, and I couldn't even think straight. My husband may have fucked a few bitches behind my back here and there, but he wasn't stupid enough to plant seeds in a bitch. He wouldn't dare do that shit to me.

"Fuck you doing going through my phone, yo? That's lame as fuck, shorty! I don't snoop around in your shit, so don't snoop around in mine!" he said, walking out of the bathroom with the towel wrapped around his waist.

He tried to come for his phone, and I swung it at his ass, damn near trying to take his head off his shoulders with it. Lucky for his sake, he'd ducked. As if everything was all good, I took a seat at the foot of the bed and crossed my leg, one over the other, rapidly bouncing it and folded my arms.

"Why are you texting a bitch named Tiana? Most importantly, why did you just send the bitch $10,000 dollars, Neo?" I calmly asked him.

You would think that I was questioning him about the weather outside by how calm my voice was.

"Ocean, let me explain this shit to you," he said.

He walked over, got down on his knees, and tried to touch me, but I pushed the shit out of him.

"Don't fuckin' touch me, nigga! Who the fuck is that bitch that you're texting? Is this the same bitch, Tiana, that you were fuckin' around on me in the past with?" I asked.

"I never fucked you and Tiana at the same time. Only

time I entertained shorty is when you put me out. I laid that shit out on the line to you, Ocean," he said to me.

"Answer my fuckin' question, Neo!" I demanded.

I knew it was going to be bullshit, which was why the tears were already falling from my eyes.

"Baby, I swear to God I'm sorry. When I landed in LA a couple months ago, Tiana hit me up and told me that she needed to talk and that it was important. I knew I shouldn't have gone, but curiosity had got the best of me, baby. Fuck, man! So, I get down there, and she tells me that we got a nine-year-old daughter—"

"Whattttt? A daughter? A daughter Neooooo? Noooo," I cried and dropped to the floor.

He came over and tried to touch me. I kicked and screamed for him to get off me, but he wouldn't. "Why would you do this? Why would you do thissss?" I cried and kept asking him over and over. "I just lost our fuckin' baby. I just lost our daughterrr. Then, ya'll name that bitch's child after our daughter? Moveeee... Neoooo moveee." I kicked for him to get off me, but he wouldn't let up.

"Fucccccckkkkk! I'm sorry, Ocean. Baby, I swear to God I'm sorry. She's nine. The shit happened when you and I were on a break," he said, on top of my body with his mouth right at my ear.

I felt wetness from him drop on me, and that's when I realized that he was crying too. I knew why he was crying. He was crying because he knew just as much as I did that this was over. Along with him knowing that he had a daughter, he had disrespected me and kept this shit from me for two fuckin' months! Looked me in my eyes and told me that nothing happened in LA when obviously a lot had happened.

Who the fuck was I even married to? How could he walk around, smile in my face, like nothing had happened, all the while he had a daughter? I cried similar to the way that I cried when I miscarried, and Neo cried right along with me. After being together almost twenty years, this was what our relationship was reduced to.

"I want a divorce, and I mean it," was the last thing I said.

If I had to spend thousands on a lawyer, I was going to do just that because there was no way I would continue to be married to a liar and a cheater. As much as I loved Neo, this was it. It was the last straw.

CHAPTER EIGHTEEN

"Babe, we have a problem," I said, walking into our bedroom and watching him as he lay in our California King sized bed wearing only his boxer briefs with his hands inside them.

God, he was so sexy. For the past few weeks, I've been putting off telling him this because I didn't want to worry him about it, but I had to say something because it was stressing me the hell out. The conversation that I had in my office a few weeks ago had been weighing heavily on my mind, especially right before she walked out, and she made that threat. I could lose my job and my license behind this. I could lose my freedom too. I thought we had everything under control and that we didn't leave any room for doubt, but Camila was on to us.

"What's the problem, babe?" he asked, sitting up in the bed and turning the television off.

I got into the bed with him, all the while, thinking to myself that I was so lucky to have gotten with a man like him. I loved everything about him from his looks to his personality, and most importantly, his heart. I've known this man for years, and we've been secretly in love for quite some time, but it wasn't always so easy to go with the way of our heart.

For years, I had to take a seat on the back burner and watch him love his fair share of women, and it was finally my turn. It was finally my turn to be in love, and I wasn't going to let nothing, or no one come between what he and I had, which was why it was so important for me to let him know what was going on with Camila. She was pressing the issue about this whole thing, and there was only so many times that I was going to be able to put her off. She had already popped up to my office after getting on a plane from Colombia. She was desperate, so there was no telling what other measures she would take to get some answers from me.

"Your wife is the problem, babe. She's on to us. She's asking too many questions. She's going to go digging for information. I know I shouldn't think about these things, but how long until she realizes that the death certificate was fake, the car crash was fake, the funeral, everything? She's not going to easily let go. I love you, but I don't want to go to prison for this," I said.

He pulled me into him and looked me in my eyes.

"Neither of us is going to prison for this. I'll handle Camila," he assured me.

"Handle her how? What are you going to do to her?" I wanted to know.

"I'm going to get rid out her. I'll get rid of anyone who is going to be a threat to what you and I have. I meant it when I said that I loved you and that I would do anything for you. *Look, I died for you,*" he said.

It was corny as hell, but I still laughed.

"You're right, Dewayne. I love you," I said, and that was that.

-To be continued

ABOUT THE AUTHOR

Hey! My name is Diamond Johnson and I'm 22 years old. I'm from Miami, Florida and I enjoy reading, especially Urban Fiction. I started reading Urban fiction when I was in the 8th grade. I knew when I was in the 10th grade that I wanted to write a book of my own and I finally did it! Some of my favorite authors and people I hope to eventually write as good as they do is Wahida Clark, Nika Michelle, and Shavon Moore. Even as a child, my elementary teacher would always tell me how much of a strong writer that I was. I'm currently attending Broward College, taking up an interest in Elementary Education. I plan to continue on with my writing, in hopes that my work will keep you guys interested and wanting more.

To my readers, I appreciate you guys so much because you keep me motivated with the positivity. Words can express the feeling I get after receiving an email from one of you, expressing how much you loved my book. By the way, feel free to add me on any of my social media pages.